WORDS
UNSPOKEN

A NOVEL

Charleston, SC
www.PalmettoPublishing.com

Words Unspoken
Copyright © 2022 by Lisa Balocca

First Edition

Paperback ISBN: 979-8-88590-883-2
eBook ISBN: 979-8-88590-898-6

WORDS UNSPOKEN

A NOVEL

LISA BALOCCA

For my daughters,
Laila and Ella.

PREFACE

This book is a work of fiction. All the characters and the situations they experience are fictitious. With that being said, several characters, as well as one or two scenes, portrayed in this book were created based on true life events but significantly altered. As I started laying the foundation, the pieces each took their own form of creation. Emma is drawn from real life, but she is not just one person. Her character is a combination of two of my closest friends. I started Delilah's character using myself as the template before she, too, took on her own characteristics and ventures. For the rest of the characters, they were created based on generality. A lot of people may know a Damon, a Blake, or even a Nick in their life, making this story a fun and relatable read.

—The Author

ACKNOWLEDGMENTS

I want to thank the one man who made me believe all things are possible, including myself. Thank you, my dearest friend Wyatt. I'd also like to thank my husband, Brett, for being the very first to read and review my work, for getting so excited about the finished product, and for encouraging me to take it as far as I can.

ONE

There he is, staring back at me. As cliché as it may sound, I'm pretty sure the world just stopped. I don't even know who he is, but for whatever reason, looking at him, I feel like I've known him my entire life. I'm not sure how, but I know he is going to be important. Can I even know that? While being all caught up in my head, I completely forget about the pool party going on around me that my best friend Emma invited me to. She has a huge backyard filled with lush green grass and tall, shady trees on one side and a fenced-in pool on the other. Right now I am standing at one end of the lawn with Emma while the handsome mystery guy is standing at the other end, leaning up against the pool fence, alone.

Emma and I have been best friends since we were basically in diapers roughly twenty-two years ago. We are pretty much sisters at this point. Even her mother considers me her second child. My parents split up when I was little. My mom is undergoing health issues, so she, for the most part, stays home. Although my wealthy grandparents dying a few years back was unfortunate, the inheritance left for my mother was very substantial. It allows for her to stay home as long as it may take for her to get strong again. Part of the money they left for her provides me with a place to live off campus while I work on college courses as well as a vehicle to get around in. As for my dad, I never knew the guy. Emma's dad died in a car accident when she was barely two years old. A car entered his lane from oncoming traffic, and to my understanding, his death was instant. Her mom is alive and well and has been inseparable from my mother since high school. They always spoke about raising their future kids together, so here we are.

Emma throws these pool parties every year and continuously throughout the warmer months. Living in Phoenix, Arizona, one can only imagine how many of those a year that can be. This is the first one kicking off the season. The water is barely warm enough to swim in. To top it all off, this one is supposed to be "the party of the year" in Emma's words. I'd be more excited, but she says that about all of them. Don't get me wrong, I love backyard pool parties as much as the next person, but the crowd can sometimes get a bit overwhelming. I've always gravitated toward the smaller group settings myself. Whenever I'm in huge social gatherings, I automatically sit back and observe everyone. Sometimes I get so caught up with it that I forget to interact, which, to be honest, I'm pretty content with. And yet there he is—shirtless if I may add—effortlessly stealing all my attention, making me wish I wasn't such a wallflower.

Even though he is standing halfway across the yard, I am positive I have never seen him before. If I had to guess, he must be the cousin Emma has told me about. She has failed to mention he is drop-dead gorgeous. He looks to stand almost six feet tall with impeccable posture. His muscles are perfectly chiseled everywhere I look, which my eyes are now making sure to cover every inch. His hair is dirty blonde and military cut, which is fitting seeing as he has recently finished his term serving in the air force. My eyes are locking in on his. Immediately, I find myself lost in their coffee-colored pools. The party, along with everyone else, is fading away as he simultaneously comes more into focus. I can't help but wonder if he is staring back because he's having similar thoughts or because maybe he's wondering who this weird girl is staring at him all goo-goo eyed.

Emma must have noticed our exchange of looks because in no time at all, she is grabbing my hand tight to pull me over to him. They grew up playing together during the summers since he was three years old and she an infant. He lived out of state, so Emma and her mom normally flew out his way. He recently moved here to be able to spend more time with Emma since they also happen to be very close.

As we are roughly five feet away from him, Emma still having a firm grip on my hand, she waves her other hand up in the air, making sure to catch his attention. This isn't hard to accomplish since his attention has remained locked on me since we were still on the other side of the yard. "Damon! Damon!" she yells. "This is my friend Delilah!"

He has an indifferent yet curious facial expression for a moment as we approach. Emma finally lets go of me and has me stand directly in front of him as she stands off to the side. He forms a smile before holding out his hand to shake mine. "I'm Damon," he says. He says nothing else as he waits for my response, making sure not to lose eye contact.

My mouth parts slightly open as I try to find words. But my nerves are leaving my mind, absent of any thoughts. Emma steps away and heads to the pool, leaving me to fend for myself. "Great," I think. I'm finally able to come up with something.

"Nice to meet you," I tell him. The moment those words leave my mouth, I scold myself quietly. "Nice to meet you! That's it? That's all you got? Moron."

It works, though, as he replies, "It's very nice to meet you. Want a drink?"

"Dos XX, extra lime, please," I reply.

"Two Dos XXs coming right up!" he says while walking away toward the cooler located just outside the back door.

I look off to the pool and see Emma staring at me, showing just about every tooth she has while giving me two thumbs-up. Blushing, I shake my head and shift my eyes to see Damon walking back my way with our drinks. Then Emma calls him over to her, forcing him to take a detour. They keep their voices low, almost on purpose, so I can't hear the conversation, not that I'd be able to hear much anyway with the distance.

I see them both glance my way, which confirms I am the topic. What are they saying? I look off just as he turns around to continue in my direction. But that only lasts for a moment as I feel compelled to look back at him. The sun is complementing his muscle definition by casting shadows in all the right places. I think some drool may have slipped out from the corner of my mouth. Thankfully, he's still too far to have noticed if so.

"Grabbed you the coldest one from the very bottom of the cooler," he says while putting it in my hand.

"Perfect," I say as I wipe off the excess ice fragments still stuck to the outside of the bottle before taking my first sip. We continue talking as we make our way to the pool to hang out with Emma. Even though she is only about a foot away from us in the water, Damon and I are too lost in conversation to alter our attention.

After a while the party is coming to an end, so we split up to help Emma clean up the mess. It's the least we can do after she put everything together. There are beer cans and empty water bottles everywhere. Thankfully, Emma's mom, Mrs. Ross, has a handle on all the food mess in the kitchen. Damon and I get so busy picking up that we forget to exchange phone numbers before leaving. But that's okay; my boyfriend wouldn't have liked it anyway.

Now when I say "boyfriend," I am using this term very loosely. It is more like a one-sided relationship to a person with commitment issues. His name—not that it's too important—is Nick. I say it's not important because I am really only holding on by a small thread made of hope to be honest. He and I have been together for one year. However, we are not officially together because he refuses to label us as anything. I won't and haven't hooked up with anyone else, and he tells me he also hasn't, but who really knows?

I bring up the "us" topic every couple of months or so. Usually, it's when he feels me pulling away and then feels the need to express just enough feelings for false hope. His argument is always the same: "Why should we have to label something? If it's real, then it's real." I always have the same response: "You should want to brag that you have me on your arm and that my eyes are only for you."

Every time we have this conversation, I can't help but think, "Why am I trying so hard to persuade him to care about me in a certain way when he obviously doesn't?" I'm aware I shouldn't be. I know that he feels how he feels and wants what he wants, and nothing I say or do can change that. I must accept it, which is exactly what I am working on. I've been having this inner battle for almost half the time we have been together, if you even want to call us that. I haven't 100 percent been closed off to new possibilities if they come knocking, but I never get past the first date. Nick usually finds out about them either through friends in common or by messaging me, asking what I'm up to. I've never lied to him. It's simply not my nature.

One time he had messaged me while I was out with a new interest, asking what I was doing. The date I was with decided to take me to this beach-themed local restaurant. Just about every table was located outside. They had their own little beach sandpit, with umbrellas mimicking the little ones found in cocktails shading each patio table. I had my phone beside my drink when I saw Nick's name pop up. I didn't plan to even open it until my date was over. But suddenly, the gentleman I was with stood up to use the restroom. Once he left his seat and walked away, curiosity got the best of me, so I grabbed my phone and read the message. I kept my response back to him quick and simple: "I am on a date."

By his immediate reply, I could tell this angered him as I read, "Possession is nine-tenths of the law."

I saw my date walking back to our table, so I sent back one final reply: "The other tenth must be me possibly meeting someone new. And you possess nothing."

With much satisfaction I slid my phone into my purse and didn't look at it for the rest of the night. I continued to be fully focused on the handsome and sweet guy I was with.

He really was wonderful, and after I got home, I lay in bed, looking forward to seeing him again.

When I woke in the morning, I first checked my phone and saw all of Nick's missed calls and texts. I decided to let him fret a bit longer before I responded to any of them. Shortly before noon I finally reached out to him. He said all the right words, giving me hope as usual. And just like that, I no longer wanted to keep pursuing the gentleman I went out with the night before. Nick had me right where he wanted me, again.

I would like to say something like this was a onetime incident, but it's, in fact, a repeating cycle. It's embarrassing. The truth is I know I deserve better, but I am also fully focused on my studies, finishing my last semester of college. I don't care to look for anyone else, nor do I even care to date at all really. At this point it's beginning to seem like I am with Nick solely for the comfort and convenience, not necessarily for the feelings that I started out with.

In the past few weeks, the dynamic I have with Nick has changed. As I feel myself becoming more distant from him, he seems to be doing the complete opposite. He has been contacting me more to come over and has been going out less with his friends, who are always on the prowl. This is obviously what I've been wanting to happen for a very long time, so why doesn't it feel right? There is something off about it. Why am I not as excited as I should be that he wants to soak up most of my free time?

He continues to come over more often, clearly heading in a more serious direction. I allow it only because I'm so confused about what's going through my head. It is such an icky feeling that I can't seem to shake. It has gotten to where I don't even care to kiss him anymore. On the other hand, this has been all I have dreamed about for the past year, so I'm not going to give up on it so easily. I need to understand this feeling more, and while I do, I'm going to give it my all one last time to see if we can finally be on the same page as far as where we stand.

TWO

It has been two weeks since I met Damon at Emma's pool party. I haven't seen or heard from him since. That is, until I see his follow request this morning on Instagram. Of course, I quickly accept the request and follow him back. Shortly after doing so, the first message from him comes through. "I enjoyed meeting you at Emma's. Hopefully I'll see you again sometime?"

I look at my phone and take a few seconds contemplating on what I want to send back. I'm obviously super attracted to him, but right now I can't offer anything but friendship. Either way, every single word I respond with matters. I decide to keep it short and simple: "Hopefully. Let's grab a drink or something sometime," adding a smiley face with my phone number. The next move is his.

On this coming weekend, Emma invites the usual group and me out for a night of karaoke. It mainly consists of a few close girlfriends of Emma's. One usually brings her live-in boyfriend along, and to be honest, I may like him more than I like her. She is nice enough, but he always comes with extremely entertaining life stories to listen to. I enjoy the rest of them quite a bit. They all have that same outgoing, extrovert personality like Emma. Even though it's the complete opposite of me, it's refreshing to be around a fun, rowdy group. It helps me break out of my comfort zone, and I always have a great time. We try to get together every week or so. Normally, it's for karaoke.

A few hours before, I see a message pop up on my phone from Nick. As usual he is wondering how I'm filling my time while I'm not with him. I respond by letting him know I'll be out with Emma. She has never really been the biggest fan of him, so I don't bring him along to these things; it wouldn't be a good mix of energy. Plus, he doesn't normally have fun with my friends anyway.

After placing the phone back down on my nightstand, I take off all my dirty clothes and throw them into the hamper before walking to my bathroom. It's only me in this one-bedroom apartment, so I don't normally have to worry about walking from one end to the other naked unless the curtains are open. But in this case, the bathroom is connected to my bedroom, so none of that would matter anyway. Waiting for the shower to get warm, I hear another text come through. I walk over to see what Nick has sent, but I see that the message is from Damon.

"What are you up to tonight? Will I be seeing you out at karaoke?" he asks.

"That you will." I respond.

"Which song do you plan on singing?" he asks.

I laugh and reply, "Ha! Ha! I don't sing."

"Aww, that's too bad," he says.

I want to send another reply, but now that I'm sure he is going to be there, I need to make myself look flawless with the couple of hours I have left. Rushing back to the shower, I spend extra time on every little task, whether it is shampooing my hair or shaving my legs, almost as if it is a ritual. I continue taking my time drying my hair and picking out my outfit even after I towel off. Tonight I decide to wear some denim shorts and a pink shirt with a sweetheart neckline. I have to throw some wedge heels in the mix to make it absolute perfection. When I finish getting ready, I take one last look at my reflection in the floor-length mirror across from my bed. I watch myself do a quick and cute back leg kick before heading out.

When I enter the karaoke lounge up the road from Emma's house, I notice that all the lights are dimmed lower than usual. I don't see any special reasoning for it, but it's nice. The walls have also been painted darker, almost a dark gray with a hint of taupe. The last time I was here, they were this bright green color, and that was only a couple of weeks ago. I, for one, like the changes. It gives the place an even more relaxing feel than it already had. The others are already here, taking turns with the microphone, keeping it away from everyone else in the bar, which by now all the usual patrons are used to. Everyone is here, that is, except for Damon, who seems to be running behind.

When they see me come up to the table, they throw the mic at me, chanting in unison, "Sing! Sing! Sing!"

"Oh, no, no, no," I say, waving my hand away at the mic.

They should know better. They try to get me up there every time, and I always refuse. Being the center of attention has never been my thing. Little do I know this time is different. Good ol' Emma, being friends with the DJ, enacted a plan before my arrival. Of course she got him involved. She's good at that. Together they had picked out a song and got their strategy in place. The DJ has the microphone and calls out my name to come and stand front and center. I'm sitting at our table, politely shaking my head no while also trying to pretend I am invisible.

Emma runs up to the DJ and grabs the mic. I then see her make her way around the room, persuading all the patrons to chant my name. Table by table she goes, and it's not long before the entire lounge is cheering me on.

I can no longer take the peer pressure. It seems the only way to make them stop is by grabbing that microphone and singing my heart out—and probably never showing my face here again afterward. "Here goes nothing!" I say as I leave the table to go put on a show one way or another.

With the mic in hand, I look up to the karaoke screen in suspense, wondering what has been chosen for me. In almost no time at all, I hear the beginning music to "Man! I Feel like a Woman!" by Shania Twain. I glance at Emma and blush as I watch for the first set of words to come up. I take a deep breath before beginning the first line, but hardly any noise comes out at all. My voice suffers more from stage fright than I am. But then the chorus happens, and my lungs find some strength. They completely open up. Emma and the rest of the group have never heard me sing before. They are looking about as shocked as I am from the sounds they hear coming from my mouth. Their jaws are literally dropped in awe.

I finish the song and look around while walking the mic back to the DJ. I notice that the rest of the patrons' faces are making the exact same facial expression as my friends. I look down a bit from all the attention as I make my way back to my seat. I glance up again briefly before sitting, and that's when I see him standing in the doorway, Damon. He is casually standing there inside the entrance door, staring at me. How long has he been there? Has he been standing there for the entire song? I take my seat as he walks over to the table.

He makes sure to say hi to me first before greeting everyone else. Then he comes closer and pulls out the empty chair next to me before taking a seat, pointing his knees in my direction. He looks at me as he brings his face even closer. Then I watch his mouth slowly open before he says, "I was mesmerized. You need to do that more often."

Instantly blushing, I take a quick glance down at his elbows that are resting on his knees before looking back into those eyes I seem to lose my words in and say, "That was a once-in-a-lifetime opportunity. Good thing you made it." We both share a small laugh as we sip on our drinks. While listening in on other conversations going on at our table, we are unable to keep from circling our attention back to each other.

Not before long, it is Emma's turn to sing again. She picks up the mic and struts to the center of the room and stares up at the screen with such confidence. Before her song comes on, she looks at me and says in a lighthearted yet threatening tone, "This one's for you! You better dance!"

Laughing, I shake my head. I look down to see Damon's hand reaching out for mine as he stands up. The moment I look up into his eyes, I am willingly at his mercy.

"Let's not disappoint her, or we'll never hear the end of it," he adamantly suggests.

He can say anything, and I'll agree to it. We share another small laugh, and then Emma gets underway singing "Strawberry Wine" by Deana Carter. I place my hand in his and allow him to lead me out to the dance floor. It's more like a designated dance section where the lounge removes a couple of tables during karaoke just for us who may want to bust a move. It's not very big, but it doesn't have to be. And besides, I prefer it that way.

When we get to the dance floor, he stops to turn and face me. It's a good thing I am so lost in his eyes because I am watching everywhere they roam. As he slowly pulls me in closer to his chest, his eyes are traveling my body from floor up until they lock with mine. He then grabs one of my hands while his other hand lightly grabs my hip, pulling me even closer. His hand slowly works its way up to my lower-mid back, where it stays. He then leads me around so gracefully and smoothly like he's done it a thousand times before. I'm sure he'd glide just as much even if this wasn't a slow song. He is sure to keep his gaze with mine.

It's not that I care much to bring him up, but I can't help but compare. One thing I really don't like when dancing with Nick is his disconnection. Whether it's me or he just doesn't like the song, his eyes almost never meet mine. They instead look past me for nearly the entire dance, probably looking for an easy opportunity, I suspect. That hound.

The song is about over, and suddenly, everyone else in the room is blurring out of the picture, just like they did at Emma's pool party. Damon is twirling me around with a huge smile on his face while the song approaches its final chord. He dips me so far down on the last beat of the song that he is on one knee. His other knee is supporting me up while he is cradling me in his arm, with the rest of him hovering over. He holds me there until the song comes to an end, and it grows silent. Then he slowly moves in and lays probably the warmest and softest kiss I've ever felt on my lips. If only it was longer.

Normally, I'd think this was moving a little too fast, but every ounce of me feels it's right. There is undeniably something else that I felt in his kiss: the chemistry, a feeling consisting of so much passion, confirming that whatever this thing is I have going on with Nick is not what I want. Whether or not Damon and I start seeing each other, never have I ever felt even a fraction of it while kissing Nick. Knowing a feeling like this exists assures me of only one thing: Nick and I are not meant to be together.

Damon and I are making our way back to the table, grinning at each other. Only a few steps away, we notice everyone gathering their things to head out. The place is closing down for the night. So we grab our belongings and walk to the door with our friends.

After we say our goodbyes to everyone, he looks at me and says firmly, "I'm walking you to your car."

"I'd like that," I say while smiling. I really like that he didn't give me a choice in the matter. We get to my car and keep talking until we are the last ones standing in the parking lot.

"Thank you for walking me out," I tell him.

Damon once again is standing in front of me while I lean my back against the driver's door of my dark blue Civic. He doesn't say anything but instead takes a step closer to me, filling the space on the ground that used to be between us. He puts both his hands on the car on each side of my head and slowly moves in for a good-night kiss. I'm expecting it this time, so I pucker up. As he pulls away to say good night, I lean in to give him one more. I then get in my car and, before driving off, look at my missed messages. Of course most are from Nick. Damon makes it back to his truck, and it's not before long that he is driving by me. While on his way to exit the parking lot with his window down, he shouts, "Your voice is amazing!"

I break out laughing before turning on my engine to head home. All I can think about is his lips. For the entire drive, I find myself smiling from ear to ear. After parking my car, I walk through the front door of my apartment, still replaying the night in my head. I can't stop thinking about that kiss. Even though it is close to midnight, my mind is still racing, and I'm not entirely mad about it. Part of the thoughts going through my head are, what am I going to tell Nick? What do I want to tell him? Whatever it is, I'll be honest as always.

Nick messages me again first thing in the morning. I keep my responses short mainly because I still don't know what I'm going to tell him. A few more messages happen back and forth before he asks if he can come over.

I say, "Okay, but there's something we need to talk about." I'm thinking these words alone will scare him off, but in almost no time at all, he is in the apartment, taking off his boots, leaving them in my doorway.

I slowly guide him to the couch in my common area as I finalize what I'm going to say. The speech in my head that I have practiced repeatedly in the mirror seems to have vanished. I hold my hands together in my lap, fidgeting with my fingernails. My palms are sweating. I haven't felt this nervous in a long time. I have no idea how to begin. So I'm going to just come out and say it. "Damon kissed me."

I look to him for a response, but he is looking at me very perplexed, not sure what to think.

I'm too anxious for there to be any silence at the moment, so I go to add, "And I kissed him back." This way it confirms it was a mutual thing and not just some random guy kissing me that I had to slap off.

He keeps looking at me, still absorbing it all. The pause in the room feels like eternity. I want to break it, but there's nothing more for me to say. He suddenly opens his mouth and hesitantly asks, "Do you like him?"

My voice trembles as I answer, "I don't know."

"Is he who you want to be with?" he asks.

My eyes fill up with tears, and I weep as I again answer, "I don't know." I can see that I am breaking his heart, but at the same time, I am wondering how that is even possible.

He takes a moment of silence while thinking of his next words. "I know a new love interest can be exciting—"

Still crying, I feel the need to interrupt him. "You know he's not the reason I'm doing this," I say while giving him a serious look.

He starts to plea. "Please, Delilah." And then I hear the words I used to long for leave his lips. "I love you."

My eyes widen for a split second before looking away. I can't even look at him any longer. With tears overwhelming my vision, I look down to the couch for them to flood out. I watch the white fabric darken in the areas the drops land. I'm not able to speak anymore, so I shake my head while still looking down. He goes to grab my hand, but I pull it away. He wraps his arms around me, pulling my head to his chest. I can practically hear his heart beating, and it's pounding.

"I love you…I love you," he continues to quietly say as I remain pressed against him.

I'm suffocating. I'm hurting him, and I can't take it. I slowly push off him and get some distance between where we are both sitting. "I can't." I sob. "It's too late. I'm sorry."

Thinking of what to say for a moment, he tells me, "I really wish you'd stay."

Pausing my sobs, I take a deep breath and respond, "You never did anything to make me want to." It's a bit harsh, but he needs to hear it.

He looks at me in disbelief before he slowly stands up, still processing our entire discussion.

"I never wanted to do this," I say as he walks over to the front door. He puts his old and worn-out boots on one by one before heading out but not before telling me he'll talk to me tomorrow. That's obviously not what I want, but I am a complete mess, so I nod slightly and tell him goodbye.

THREE

The sun is beaming in through my blinds, aimed directly at my face. It's morning. I slowly open my eyes, but I'm not ready to get up. I'm just going to lie here for a bit. The past two days with Damon and then Nick keep running through my mind. How am I feeling right now? Confused. Damon sparks this fire in me that I really want to explore. The chemistry between the two of us is undeniably intense. But this past year with Nick and being distracted in my studies make me want to focus only on friends and school for the moment. I need to find myself again, my individuality. I'm not sure what I want with Damon at this point, but I do know I need to do my own thing for a while and put my love life on hold. Today is going to be a me day. No boys, no friends, just me. But first, I need to move from this bed. I lean over to my bedside table to grab my phone. Then I begin checking all my notifications.

Nick messaged me about an hour ago. "Good morning, beautiful." I keep holding the phone for a moment while I stare at his message. Flashbacks from the entire year flood my mind. I immediately put it back down without responding. I'm not looking at that for the rest of the day. I walk to the kitchen to grab some fresh morning coffee before working on my course assignments. I'm currently a full-time student working on a criminal justice degree. All my classes are online and accelerated, so I can hopefully get done in half the time. I normally do summer courses as well, so I can stay on pace for my goal of graduating after this semester.

I don't currently hold a full-time job, but I do have a part-time internship at the Arizona Attorney General's Office. They only give me two or three shifts a week, so it almost isn't even worth mentioning. The internship is paid, though, not that I need it to make rent or anything else due to my mom's generous donation from her inheritance. Working my butt off all those years in school actually paid off because I have a full-ride college scholarship based on my prior grades. A bonus is the distraction that all this schoolwork gives me from everything else in life, including boys. The relief is actually addicting.

Two weeks later I'm still in my apartment, studying—with breaks, of course. But I haven't really been out too much. Nick keeps messaging me and giving me the random phone call. Sometimes I will answer his texts to be nice, keeping my responses brief. Damon has also been messaging me, wanting to see me again and not just at the weekly dinners we have at Emma's house. I truly look forward to those, and knowing he is going to be there gets me even more excited. She knows I live alone, and Damon is new here, so she tries to have us over as much as possible. Honestly, I think it's really to get Damon and me together, but I'll continue to play dumb for now. To have two of her favorite people end up together would probably be a dream come true for her. As captivated as he and I seem to be with each other every time we're together, I've been making excuses to put off one-on-one time not because I want to but because I just feel like I need to breathe my own air for a bit. Besides, I still have Nick kind of hanging around, and I don't want to get Damon involved in any of that.

Knock...knock...knock! Who could that be? It's dinnertime and I'm not expecting anyone. I walk over to my front door and look out the peephole and see Nick standing there. My eyes grow big as I carefully step away from the door and across the common area until my back bumps against the kitchen counter. Maybe he doesn't know I'm here. My heart beats faster, and I feel my breath become shallow. He has never once paid me a surprise visit. Why is he here? Even though he has never had a key, I still feel as though I am trapped.

I quietly creep around the apartment to find a small crack in the blinds to watch him. He is standing in the entryway, fiddling with his phone for a moment longer, before I hear his key chain jingle as he steps away. I wait for another minute to make sure he's gone. A couple of minutes later, I am able to relax a little bit. After I finally hunt down my phone that has been on vibrate since this morning, I see four missed calls from him, which he made while he was standing outside my apartment. There's no way I'm responding. In fact, I am done sending back any messages. He shouldn't come over uninvited.

Three days later a text from Damon catches my attention: "Hey! Are you busy? I want to take you shooting at the gun range."

Great. I am now battling between finishing a paper and going shooting with someone I haven't been able to stop thinking about. "I'm free!" I respond.

"Wait," I tell myself. I haven't even made up my decision yet if I want to go. I guess it's too late because he is on his way over.

Knock…knock…knock! I hesitantly look up at the door, a little unsure about who it might be. Although I have a pretty good idea who to expect, I'm still rattled by Nick showing up the other night. Then I hear someone say, "Your chariot awaits, my lady!" I know that voice—Damon.

"I'll be right there!" I shout.

Grabbing my things, I then open the door. I see him, and he looks effortlessly perfect. He is wearing dark blue jeans, a white shirt, and the most charming grin. Taking a deep breath, I follow him down the narrow hallway toward his silver truck, making sure not to take my eyes off him. He can walk in front of me all day as far as I'm concerned, and if he happens to drop something in front of him, causing him to bend over to pick it up, that's OK too—very OK actually.

He opens the passenger door and waits for me to get in before closing it. On the entire way there, he is asking me questions left and right. He asks how many siblings I have, and I tell him I'm an only child. His other questions include my interests and favorite food and music. I try to answer as many as I can while also asking him some of my own. We arrive to the outdoor gun range and have a lot of fun with even more laughs. I can shoot decently, but it is not even close to the skills he learned during his time serving in the military. He gets the bull's-eye just about every time. My shots, for the most part, remain a little off-center.

He watches me fire a couple of more rounds before placing his Glock down on the table in front of him and saying,
"Put down your gun. I want to show you something."

Curious about what it could be, I laid mine down beside
his. He goes behind me and carefully adjusts my posture
to achieve a better shooting stance. His lips come up to
my ear, saying, "This is the position I want you in," before
taking a step back, giving me a wink.

Blushing ever so slightly, I laugh nervously and reply,
"Yeah, yeah. Are you going to stand there all day or hand
me my gun?"

He laughs while placing it in my hands and says,
"Now shoot."

The next two shots I fire nearly hit the bull's-eye. I look
at him and see he is just as excited for me as I am. Once I
fire my last round, I then turn around to catch him staring
at me. "Are you hungry?" he asks.

"Starving," I reply.

He then asks, "Where should we go?"

"Hmmm." I think for a second. "I make the best grilled
cheese sandwiches."

"Your place it is," he says with a smile.

We head out of the range, and he again opens his truck
door for me. I'm such a sucker for chivalry. We get back to
my place, and I have him sit on the couch while I make my
way to the kitchen. He is still watching me as I pull all the
ingredients out onto the counter and get to work.

Then my phone starts blowing up. It's Nick. I will not
deal with him right now. I place my phone on the counter
so I can see any more incoming calls. But instead of seeing a third call coming through, he messages me, saying

he is on his way over. At least he gives me a warning this time, but shit! I quickly make my way around the apartment, locking all the doors and closing all the blinds and curtains, trying not to make it look obvious. But how can it not? Miraculously, Damon doesn't catch on, or at least he doesn't ask what I'm doing. In all our conversations, we have yet to have the awkward ex talk.

The sandwiches are finally done. Damon and I sit down to eat. There still hasn't been a knock on the door, thank goodness. Maybe I can breathe again. He is done eating, and out of fear of Nick possibly still showing up, I keep the rest of the visit short. We walk toward the door, and as I go to open it, Damon closes it again and looks at me. He takes one of his hands and runs it through my hair before trailing my jawline toward my mouth. He holds my chin, bringing it closer to his, and gives me another slow kiss. This one lasts much longer than our first three at the karaoke lounge a few weeks back. I feel like I'm hovering slightly off the floor. Our mouths slowly pull apart as gravity sets back in. My feet are still on the ground after all. He opens the door and tells me goodbye, leaving me to crave for more.

I lock the door behind him and take a deep sigh, feeling like I'm floating in the clouds again. A few moments later, I remember that Nick still might be on his way. I abruptly fall out of the sky and back to the earth. What am I doing? I don't want to be involved with anyone. Heck, I'm still trying to get rid of the last one!

I head into the kitchen to clear the lunch mess and check my phone. There is nothing from Nick, but I do see a missed call from Emma, followed by a text. She wants to go get pedicures. That's a great excuse for not being home if he comes by, so I reply, "On my way!" I can use some girl time after what happened.

Arriving at the nail salon, I see her standing outside the front door, flagging me down. She has already had them prefill two pedicure chair basins with the suds we each like. Emma's go-to is always green tea, and mine is usually whatever fruity scent they have at the time. Today it's peach, my favorite. We take our spots next to each other and catch up on our daily gossip. She listens with little input as I tell her what's been going on with Nick. I refrain from mentioning anything about Damon, not that I think she'd mind at all; she's practically pushing us together. I guess I just don't want her to get involved in any way. I want to keep whatever is going on between Damon and me separate from me and her. Suddenly, I drift from conversation, entering a daze, not realizing it at first. I am, without a doubt, daydreaming of Damon.

"What color do you want for your toe?" the nail technician asks while massaging my calves.

I snap out of my trance. "Er...uh...pink," I answer. Gosh, this pedicure is nice. I can use a nap after this.

Emma and I give each other a big hug before leaving. "Love you!" Emma shouts as she waves her hand while getting into her car.

I shout back, "Love you more!" as I do the same.

I park my car in my covered spot at the apartment complex, and before getting out, Nick and Damon enter my thoughts. I continue to sit there as I think of how close they came to meeting face-to-face and possibly having a confrontation. Whether I choose to pursue Damon or not, Nick must go.

I finally get out of my car and close the door. As I walk down the hallway, I see a mountain of gifts neatly placed on my welcome mat. Attached to a bouquet of flowers is a card. Even though I already know who it is from, I open it anyway. Of course, it's from Nick. This isn't good. I need to get rid of these stat. I think of throwing them out, but I don't want him thinking I have kept them. So instead, I pile the lot in my car and take it all to a friend's house of his, planning to dump it off on the doorstep.

When I get to the street that his friend lives on, I see Nick's gold truck parked out front on the asphalt right off the driveway. I immediately hatch a better plan as I slow my vehicle while I approach. My adrenaline is pumping as I look over my steering wheel, scoping out the area. I don't see him or his friend in sight, so I pull up beside his truck and transfer everything over into the bed as fast as I can. I quickly hop in my car and drive off, peeling around the street corner to the main road, laughing to myself. Other drivers passing me by are probably thinking I must be having some sort of nervous breakdown, but I don't care. That was awesome, and I'm completely satisfied with myself.

It doesn't take him long to notice what I did because, in no time at all, I receive a text from him asking about it. "Did you drop these off?" he asks.

"I did," I reply. "I need you to stop coming over."

"I want to still be your friend," he responds.

Obviously knowing he has ulterior motives, I can't let him stay in my life. He will never leave me alone and move on if I do. "I'm not able to be that to you right now," I type before pressing Send. And just so he knows I'm serious, I block his number as well as all his social media accounts.

FOUR

It's been over a month since I've last heard anything from Nick. Damon and I have been consistently seeing each other roughly once or twice a week outside of meeting at Emma's for dinner. We talk just about every day on the phone. Even though things are progressing between us, we've been moving slow while I figure out what exactly I want this to turn into. I'm definitely sure I want him around, but to what extent? He has remained a patient gentleman throughout this entire process while I hope for things to just fall into place. My thoughts lately have been siding more with wanting to be with Damon over anything. Neither of us has stayed the night at each other's places, nor have we even gone past second base. I would be lying if I say that there weren't times we were headed for more, but I thankfully still have enough willpower to hold back, though nothing about him makes it easy.

Friday afternoon approaches, and I'm wrapping up my schoolwork for the week when I receive a call from Damon. He wants to take me out to dinner. Apparently, it's a really nice place, judging from how he describes it. Trying to hold in my excitement, I tell him I'll be ready in two hours. Immediately, I toss my books to one side and slide my computer out of my lap to the other. I then hop out of my recliner, sprinting to the shower to get ready. I'm so excited that I feel like I'm moving at warp speed and for no reason whatsoever; it's not like I'm running out of time.

After rinsing all the soapsuds off, I quickly wrap the towel around my body and step out of the shower. I'm entirely oblivious to the water trail I leave while making my way across the bathroom to my closet. I have enough dresses to suit any and every occasion, yet I can't seem to find one good enough for tonight. After trying on about half my closet, I see a little number in the back with the tag still on—perfect.

I bought this dress on the Strip while visiting Las Vegas with Emma. It looked gorgeous hanging on the manne- quin displayed in the boutique's window. It has a beautiful powder blue color with a swoop neck complimented by an elegant lace accent. As the dress lured me into the store to try it on, I already knew it was going to be the perfect fit. Emma refused to let me leave without it once she saw it on me. Now looking back, I'm so glad she practically blocked the exit.

Stepping into the dress one foot at a time, I slowly shimmy it up, putting my arms through the sleeves that drape just off my shoulders. Yup, it still fits the same as the day I tried it on, hugging all my curves, flattering my hourglass figure. It cuts off just above my knees. I find the perfect clear-colored stilettos to make my toned legs pop and give me a few extra inches in height. Let's face it, I'm only 5'2". The higher the heel, the better. Next, the hair. My hair is dark, is naturally straight, and has grown down to barely skim my waist. Normally, I don't do much to it, but tonight is different. I am curling the hell out of it. While I'm putting the final touches, there's a knock at the door.

Before opening it, I look through the peephole to make sure it's Damon. I open the door, and there he is, bringing out a single red rose from behind his back. He must take me for a sucker, which I totally am. Before heading out, I invite him inside while I run into the kitchen to pull out a vase from the cupboard. Filling it up with cold water, I place the rose inside and set it on my nightstand before taking a deep sniff of its sweet scent. I feel my heart warm in my entire chest and look back at Damon. "OK, let's go!"

We arrive to the valet area of the restaurant and hand off our keys before walking inside. The host shows us to our reserved table covered with a white tablecloth and napkins to match. Dinner is absolutely amazing. He made sure to get the table with the best view. Staring at him and this cotton-candy-colored sky is so settling and romantic. Arizona truly has the most giving sunsets. As the check comes and our empty plates are taken away, we sip on our cabernet, still gazing at the abstract picture painted in the sky. The pinks and oranges are keeping my attention while he veers in my direction. I take a deep breath before letting it out to say, "So breathtaking."

Damon reaches his hand across the table, placing it on top of mine as he says, "You really are." And just like that, the sunset loses its hold on me. I look at him and smile with absolutely nothing to say. He has pleasantly caught me off guard with that one.

Seconds later here comes our server with the receipt. Damon signs before saying, "Let's get out of here."

During the drive back to my place, I am trying to concentrate on sitting still while I'm feeling over giddy. I glance over at him, hoping to get a similar read, but he looks so calm and collected. Once I direct him to park in the visitor section, he gets out. Then he comes around to the passenger side to open his truck door for me like he usually does without fail. He interlocks my fingers with his while we walk up to the front door.

As I slide my key into the lock, he gives me a good-night kiss. Or at least I think that's what it is. He begins kissing me harder. I'm still trying to open the door, but he's not making it easy, and I'm not complaining. Finally, I find the doorknob and open it as we stumble our way inside. His lips still haven't left mine. He has me standing with my back up against the wall just inside the doorway. One of his hands is holding my back, and the other is sliding up through my hair. He intertwines my hair with his fingers and pulls my head back toward the wall while his mouth softly moves from mine down to my neck. He releases my hair and moves down to one of my shoulders while his other hand trails up my back to find my other shoulder. He pushes my sleeves lightly, dropping my dress down to the floor. He stops kissing my neck for a moment and takes a step back to get a good look at me practically standing naked in front of him.

Then he takes off his shirt over his head in what I view as slow motion. His muscles are all so defined. I caress his chest and arms, feeling every curve. He goes back to kissing my lips as his hands find their way under my butt, lifting me off the floor. I wrap my legs around him while he carries me to my room.

We don't stop kissing until he lays me on the bed with him on top. He slips off my panties before kicking off his pants. His face is only inches from mine; he looks into my eyes as his groin brushes up against me. Slowly at first, he works his way fully inside me. I can't stop myself from letting out a gasp while I lean my head back on my pillow. He kisses my neck, working down to my breast. Twirling his tongue around my nipple at first, he takes me into his mouth, moving from one breast to the other. He enters me faster and faster while we are both about to climax. As my lips form to orgasm, his mouth finds mine, muffling my moan. We continue kissing until we both finish. Then we peel our mouths apart and lay there, looking into each other's eyes a moment longer before closing them to fall asleep.

Rolling over to the other side of the bed this morning, I don't feel him beside me. The sheets also feel cold. I prop myself up, looking around the room. Before any thoughts come to my mind, I hear his voice from the kitchen.

"Do you want banana or blueberry pancakes?" he shouts.

Taking a sigh of relief, I smile. "Blueberry!" I respond.

"And coffee?" he then asks.

"Black with a dallop of honey," I respond. A few minutes later, he is bringing me breakfast in bed. He kisses my forehead before placing the tray down in front of me. "Wow, this looks amazing!"

"Oh, it's nothing," he says. "Wait until you see what I can do in my kitchen."

I look at him and smile before grabbing another bite off my plate. He finishes up his pancakes and takes our dirty dishes into the kitchen. Meanwhile I rush out of bed, heading straight to the bathroom to fix this mess I call hair. I come out to see him gathering his things together.

"I have some things I need to get done this morning," he says regrettably.

Although curious about what he means, I choose not to pry but instead say, "Oh, OK, absolutely!"

"Are you going to be at karaoke tonight?" he then asks.

"I was a little too preoccupied to think about it," I say flirtatiously.

He laughs agreeably. "I'll pick you up at six."

"OK," I say, secretly jumping up and down inside. He comes close slowly for one more long kiss before closing the door to my apartment behind him.

Wow. Being involved with him is something I can easily get used to. All I can think about is seeing him later this evening. I need to do something to fill my time; otherwise, I'll sit here and daydream all day. Well, I'm surely not doing any schoolwork on a Saturday. Contemplating for a moment, I decide that shopping it is. I take a trip to the local mall and find the perfect little black dress to wear tonight. This time I'll leave out the heels and wear my black flats with jewels for that extra pizazz.

After getting home from shopping, I feel exhausted, so I make myself a late lunch before taking a catnap. Probably not too far away from drooling on the pillow, I wake up to a text from Damon. "On my way!" it reads.

I rub my face as I'm still half asleep before looking at the time. Shrieking, I see that it's already five thirty! I jolt up and fly through the house, putting myself together in what is probably a world record. I get done only minutes before he knocks on the door.

"You look stunning," he says while looking at me wide-eyed.

I nervously laugh as I respond, "Oh, this? Please, it only took me ten minutes to throw this together." It honestly did as I was frantically racing the clock. He leans in to kiss me before leading the way out down the narrow hallway.

We are the last in our group to arrive to the karaoke lounge. Emma and everyone watch as we make our way in, holding hands. We get to our table and begin our greetings. I go to say hi to Emma and see her wearing the giddiest grin while shifting her eyes from Damon to me and then back. Damon sits down while I finish my round of hugs. As I go to pull out my seat beside him, he puts his hands on my hips, pulling me down to sit on his lap.

"This is a much better spot," I say to him and laugh while looking for our server to place our drink order. We haven't seen one come by in a while, not that I'm surprised; the place is unusually packed tonight. A few minutes later, I stand up to go over to the bar since I still haven't seen a server anywhere. After I place our order to the bartender, I look past him and see Nick sitting on the other side.

He has his arms overlapping on the counter with a drink in his hand, looking at me. He looks to be alone. I'm trying to avoid eye contact as I wait for the bartender to finish up with my drinks, but Nick won't stop staring. It is almost making me nervous. Why does he look so angry? Why is he here? It's not totally unusual since he does frequent this place from time to time but normally not on karaoke nights, which makes this a bit unsettling.

The bartender places the order in front of me. I quickly grab the drinks and head back to my table. I hand Damon's to him before he opens up his arms, signaling for me to take my place back on his lap. After doing so, I take a sip of my drink, and out of curiosity, I look at Nick from the corner of my eye. He has a clear view of Damon and me. I can see the reason for his annoyance, but that's not my problem. He doesn't move from his spot but continues watching us. I feel really uncomfortable, so I move from Damon's lap to my own chair.

Damon then looks over to me and sees me glancing up to the bar. "Everything OK?" he asks.

"Yes," I reply. I unintentionally glance at Nick one more time to see if he's still watching; he is.

Damon notices Nick's piercing stare and asks, "Who is that guy?"

I still haven't mentioned anything about Nick to him. I'd like to think I have it under control. I don't want Damon seeing him as a threat in any way because what I want in life simply does not involve Nick. Plus, before tonight it had been weeks since I've seen or heard from him, so why bring anything up? I decide to respond, "Some creep apparently."

Damon has his guard up a little bit, but he's not letting Nick ruin his night. I, however, feel uneasy. My lungs feel as though they are getting smaller as I quietly gasp for air. Now I feel like I'm being stalked. What is Nick trying to accomplish? A restraining order? I should be able to enjoy my time without looking over my shoulder and have a love life without feeling like it's wrong. I guess Nick can't take seeing me with Damon anymore because he closes his tab and walks out. When he gets to the exit, he turns around, looking at us both one last time before leaving, and of course, Damon notices.

The room suddenly fills back up with air, and I can breathe again. We all continue on as usual, and Damon doesn't mention "the creep" for the rest of the night. Meanwhile, my mind is racing with thousands of thoughts. What is Nick's next move? How far will he go? I've never seen him desperate like this. Should I tell Damon about him? Should I put things on hold with Damon until Nick is gone for good?

When the karaoke festivities end, Damon drives me back home. While in his truck, I look over to see him unduly focused on the road. Something is on his mind, and I'm pretty sure I know what that thing is, Nick. Once we park in my complex, he gets out of the driver's side and rounds the hood to come and open my door. He's not smiling his usual smile. It's smaller with a hint of concern. I smile at him, pretending not to notice, while he walks me down the hallway to my front door to say good night. We get to the welcome mat, and I see him pull a note off the door as I'm digging for my keys in my purse. He then holds it up with one hand while looking at me.

"May I?" he asks.

Curious yet hesitant, I reply, "Sure, go ahead." After all, I have nothing to hide.

He continues to unfold it. After looking at the note for a moment, he looks at me with a facial expression owning a thousand questions. But instead of asking a single one of them, he places the note in my hand, gives me a quick kiss, and heads back to his truck. My heart drops a little; this is not his normal goodbye. Once he's out of sight, I look down to the note in my hand and read, "You looked beautiful tonight. New dress?" It's not signed by Nick, but it doesn't have to be for me to know he's the one who left it. And I'm pretty sure Damon is smart enough to figure that out also.

My heart beats fast as I look around for Nick outside the doorway to my apartment. Even though I don't see him, I'm panicking. I quickly unlock the door, get inside, and lock the dead bolt. Needing to sit down, I make my way over to the couch and focus on my breath, slowly breathing deeply in and out, until my heartbeat settles back down to its normal rhythm.

Now that I can think straight again, I need to talk to Damon. I must tell him everything. He's probably so confused. I message him, "Are you free tomorrow? I want to see you." But he doesn't respond.

He messages me late in the morning. "Let's see a movie later."

Oh, thank goodness. "That sounds great," I reply. We won't get the chance to discuss things at the movie, but I'm just glad he is willing to see me. Maybe we can talk in the truck on the way there or back.

Damon arrives at seven o'clock, just in time. I open the door to see him smiling that bright, white smile like yesterday never happened. He gives me a kiss before walking me to his truck and opening the door. Once buckled up, he searches for my hand and holds it for the entire drive. The whole way to the movie theater, we are busy talking about so many other subjects that the one on Nick never comes up. He never even asks about it. But I can still tell he has something on his mind. The same thing happens when it's time to come back from the movie; we are too busy discussing our favorite scenes. By the time we get back to my apartment, it's fairly late.

"Would you like to come in?" I ask before I head inside through the doorway.

He keeps his reply short. "Not tonight." Then he gives me another quick kiss and leaves as I remain confused.

Once I'm inside my apartment, I get ready for bed while trying to wrap my head around everything. Have I ruined it with Damon? He seems to be backing off and not as interested in pursuing me anymore. But then why did he bother taking me out? He is being too hot and cold for my taste.

Monday came and went, and the week goes on; I have barely heard anything from Damon. He messaged me once, asking if he left his sunglasses in the house; he didn't, and I haven't heard anything else from him. I wonder if he'll even be at the karaoke this Saturday. For the next two days, I try to put him as far from my mind as possible.

Saturday has come, and still not hearing a word from Damon, I end up driving myself to the karaoke lounge. Everyone is here besides him. I'm not exactly upset about it since I have zero clue on what is going on between us. Roughly about five songs later, I look up and see Damon sitting at the bar with a young and attractive woman. I glance at Emma and everyone else, but I don't think any of them realize he is here. I watch him for a moment longer and see him lean in closer to her, smiling that smile I've grown so fond of. Then the hurt and anger sets in. Of all places, he chooses to bring her here?

I look away from him before he can catch my stare and realize anything. The last thing I want is for him to see me affected by any of his actions. I figure, why give him that luxury? Poker face it is. But wait, I'm affected? These feelings I have been trying not to feel for him become undeniable. I want him, he is all I want, and I am certain. I question how I let myself push him away. I didn't mean to when I was uncertain in the beginning about being with anyone. If it's because of Nick being a creep the last time we were here, then all I have to do is explain, and he'll understand everything. I feel so stupid; how could I allow this to happen?

A couple of more songs and one more drink later, I'm ready to leave. I bid Emma and everyone goodbye and tell them that I'll see them next week. Damon doesn't even glance at my direction as I walk out the door.

The very next Saturday comes around, and I still haven't heard a word from Damon. Emma calls and decides to come over to my place for half the day before karaoke. We lie out by the office pool for a bit before heading back to my unit located at the other end of the complex. There is a pool only a few feet away from my apartment, but it isn't as big, and it certainly doesn't have a built-in waterfall like this one. After Emma and I get ready for karaoke, we go out to grab a bite to eat on the way to the lounge. Our server runs behind on grabbing our check, so we are the last ones to the karaoke lounge, not that I'm mad about it.

Once we walk in, I see Damon sitting at the table with everyone this time, and his arm is around a completely different girl from last week. Again, I pretend to not be fazed by his player behavior, but I am honestly tearing apart inside. We have been seeing each other for weeks; how can he toss me aside so suddenly? I take my seat by Emma across from Damon. He watches me sit down before look-ing away in an attempt to ignore me.

"What is your name?" I ask his flavor of the week.

He looks at me nervously while she responds, "Oh, I'm Keesha."

"Nice to meet you, Keesha. I'm Delilah," I say before glancing at Damon, who looks like he's about to break out in sweats. He can relax though. I won't say anything. I'd rather watch her cycle through like the one last week, like me.

I stay for a few more songs, but I don't really care to stick around longer than I have to. So I again say my goodbyes and leave but not before Emma catches my arm. "Delilah, you're going to be at the pool party tomorrow, right?" she asks.

"You know I wouldn't miss it," I tell her.

"Good, you better not!" she threatens as I leave.

I'm about an hour late to the pool party. I sneak in so Emma doesn't notice me. As I head to the cooler, I hear someone stomp up behind me.

"There you are!" Emma shrieks.

"Sorry." I laugh as I jump. "I couldn't decide what to wear."

"Whatever," she says. "Grab a drink and get your party on."

"Yes, ma'am!" I respond as she walks away to her next victim. I continue to open the cooler lid and pull out a beer. Just as I look at a nearby table for a bottle opener, a good-looking guy walks up to pop the cap off for me.

"Just the man I needed." I tell him. He laughs before starting conversation. We've been having small talks for a bit when I see Damon enter the party, surprisingly with no new woman in his arm. In almost no time at all, he looks my way, and I can see him turn into a green, jealous monster, not that I meant for this to happen, but he can take his medicine.

The good-looking guy and I part ways moments after, and I walk inside to the kitchen for pizza. Damon comes in behind me and tries everything to get my attention without being obvious. It is obvious, though, so I make sure not to give in. He walks across two more times, pretending to do things on each side of the room. Then he walks right up to me and doesn't say anything while leading me into an empty common area that is divided off the kitchen by a wall.

"Yes, Damon?" I ask.

"What are you doing here with him?" he asks.

"Why do you care?" I say. "And I am not with him. Why are you with different women every week?"

"Because you're involved with that guy who was staring at you that night at karaoke," he accuses.

"No, I'm not," I say defensively. "He was someone I used to be involved with. Seriously, Damon, why didn't you just ask?"

He paces around the room for a moment before telling me to grab my stuff. "Why? Where are we going?" I demand.

"I want to be alone with you," he says. "Let's go grab dinner?"

"Oh, you think it's that simple?" I ask, about to decline the invitation.

Annoyed, he answers, "Those girls meant nothing, Delilah."

"Oh, and I do?" I question.

"Yes," he replies without a single stutter.

Pausing to think for a moment, I respond, "Fine," before changing my clothes and grabbing my things. We get in his truck and go to a hole-in-the-wall down the street. We don't touch the topic of seeing other people but instead try to act as if none of it ever happened.

When we're done eating, he offers to take me home and drive me back to my car in the morning. I feel like we have some catching up to do, and a quick dinner is not satisfying enough, so I tell him yes. We get back to my apartment and walk inside.

After taking off our shoes, I head to the bathroom to get ready for bed. I look for a spare toothbrush in the medicine cabinet and see Damon through the mirror coming up behind me. Suddenly, one of his hands grab hold of my waist, pulling it toward him, and the other pushes down on my back until I am bent over the bathroom counter. I knock his hands off, but he continues to keep a firm hold of my waist while his other hand is now running up the inside of my leg. His fondling is getting me so aroused. I try to stand up, but then his hand pushes me back down to the counter before unzipping his pants. He then places both hands on my hips and, in one swift motion, enters me. He starts out going fast, then harder and harder, almost aggressively. But again, I'm not complaining. My hands are gripping the counter so hard that they're cramping as they slip. His breathing then becomes deeper and more rhythmic. He thrusts a couple of more times before pulling out, finishing in his hands, with the excess slipping through his fingers onto the floor.

I then lead us into the shower where there is a lot more kissing than actual washing. However, with the way his hands are rubbing all over me, I could have been fooled otherwise. Once we are dry, we don't even bother getting dressed. Instead, we crawl with our naked bodies under the sheets and call it a night while I lay my head on his chest.

Damon is acting interesting again the next morning, but in a different way. He is just lying in my bed, staring up at the ceiling, not saying a word. His mind seems heavy judging from how hard he is focusing on the fan blades. They're not even moving at the moment. I'm sure there is something on his mind. But I'm not so positive if it's still Nick.

"Is everything OK?" I ask.

"Yeah," he replies while not breaking eye contact with the fan.

I stare at him for a moment. Why is he being so quiet? I'm trying to think of words to provoke a conversation, any type of conversation at this point. But I am so thrown off at his change of demeanor that once again I'm speechless.

He suddenly receives a phone call that lasts for only a minute tops. Once he hangs up, he looks at me with the same focused expression he's had all morning. "I need to go."

"Are you sure everything is OK?" I ask.

"Yes. Fine," he replies. "I'll take you back to your car."

"OK," I say. The car ride is mostly quiet with some small talk here and there.

"I'll see you at karaoke this coming weekend, right?" he asks while I get out of his truck.

I think, "A whole week this time before I see him again?" It's not the end of the world, but it's also not the usual pattern we had before.

I answer back, "I plan on being there."

Throughout the week Damon and I keep in contact every day, but the communication is different. Our conversations could last for several hours a day before, but now it has turned into a few short texts here and there. What's the main difference that I notice? He has stopped wanting to get to know me. All his endless questions about my likes and dislikes, favorite childhood memories, and hobbies have stopped. I sigh as I lay my face in my palm; I knew I should have just focused on myself and not gotten involved with anyone. On a more positive note, it's the end of the week. All I have is one paper left, and my weekend can begin.

Saturday finally presents itself. With how long this week has been, the day couldn't have come fast enough. I arrive at our karaoke spot and see Emma's hand up in the air, showing me where they are seated. She's just about to head to the floor to sing. As I take steps toward our table, I notice that Damon is not sitting there. I glance to the bar in case he is putting an order in. He isn't up there either, but Nick sure is.

Stopping in my tracks, I bite my bottom lip for a moment and decide I've had enough. It's time to confront him. I march over to where Nick is standing and begin to tear into him. "What are you doing?" I demand.

"Well, right now I'm trying to order another round," he replies in the cockiest way.

"Why here? Why are you coming here?" I ask.

He looks at me for a moment and answers, "It's a public place, is it not? I can be here if I want."

I hesitantly ask, "Why do you want to be?"

He gives me a good long stare. "You," he says while he steps to my side, putting his arm around me. "I know you still love me. Let me take you home, and we can pretend this whole breakup thing never happened."

His hand creeps up my arm toward my shoulder, about to pull me in. I turn to face him, purposely slipping it off back to his side. I look up to meet his eyes with mine, but before I can say anything to him, I see Damon in my peripheral vision standing across the lounge, watching us, and he does not look happy.

I stop what I am doing and turn to walk toward Damon. But before I can take a step, he walks back out the door, leaving the lounge. Infuriated, I look up at Nick and yell, "You were nothing but a waste of time and energy! You will never be able to have me again!"

I turn around and run out the front door leading to the parking lot in search of Damon to explain everything. As I look through the car aisles, I don't see him anywhere. I walk between two cars heading toward another aisle to look. I shout his name several times before I feel a hand on my shoulder, turning me around. "Thank goodness," I think. But when I turn around, expecting to find Damon, I see Nick. He seems to be way more drunk than he appeared to be inside.

"I'll never be able to have you again, huh?" he mumbles while staggering forward, almost falling on me.

I take a step back, and he lunges at me, forcing me to scream. He shoves my back against a random parked car, pinning me in place. Shocked for a moment by his aggressiveness, I hit him over and over, crying for help, but no one is outside to hear me. He wraps one hand around my throat, then pulls me off the car before throwing me to the ground. He climbs on top of me as I attempt to scream again. But he covers my mouth with one hand while ripping my jeans with the other. I keep trying to squirm free, but his strength is too overpowering.

About to give up and let him have his way with me, I see an arm come around his neck from behind, pulling him off. Both men fall backward to the ground and struggle while Nick tries to break free. I sit up and see it is Damon! Damon squeezes his arm around Nick's neck even tighter. I see Nick's face turn bright red before he passes out, dropping his head to the ground.

Damon then stands up and walks over to me. "Are you OK? Are you hurt?" he asks, wearing a concerned expression.

With my voice shaking, I say, "I'm fine." In all honesty, I am anything but fine. Besides probably needing therapy, I have bruises already appearing from being tossed around. He pulls me up to my feet, holding me in his arms, before calling the police. His arms are around me so tight that I feel like my lungs are collapsing. I'm starting to have trouble breathing, but this time it's in the best way.

I tell Damon everything about Nick while we wait for the police to show up. The officer who arrives to the scene is tall with broad shoulders and quite intimidating. He walks over to us as we stand by Nick, who is now sitting up but still on the ground. Damon has not let him out of his sight. As the officer is only three feet away, I can read his badge, "Officer Jones."

He sees Nick on the ground and comes to stand slightly closer to him while he gathers the complete story. He first asks, "Is everyone OK?"

I'm still processing the trauma, so Damon speaks for me while pulling me in even tighter. "We are, thankfully."

Officer Jones looks down at me for a long moment before asking our names. I slowly look up into his dark green eyes and say, "He is Damon, and I'm Delilah."

"That's a beautiful name," he says. "Would you mind telling me everything that happened, Delilah?"

"OK," I reply. I have his complete attention as I tell him every detail. Shortly after, he grabs hold of Nick's arm, standing him up, before putting his hands in cuffs behind his back, walking him over to his patrol car, and placing him in the back seat. Officer Jones then says a few words into his police radio before getting in his vehicle and driving away. I sigh with relief. "He's gone...Nick's gone."

Damon finally loosens his death grip and says, "Leave your car here tonight. I'm taking you home." I've never needed him to say that more than now.

FIVE

In the morning Damon takes me back to the karaoke lounge to grab my car. We get out of his truck and walk to mine hand in hand. Before he gives me a kiss goodbye, he looks at me regrettably and says, "There's something I've been needing to talk to you about. Can we get together tonight?"

My chest sinks. There is nothing else I can say other than "OK. Dinner? My place?"

"Sure, that sounds good," he says. "I'll see you around six o'clock."

"Sounds great," I say with a smile that is hiding how much I'm freaking out. He gives me a kiss before closing my car door behind me.

I haven't looked at my phone ever since leaving the karaoke lounge last night, so I sit for a moment in my car to catch up. There are missed calls from Emma, followed by a text: "Are you OK? Where did you go? I saw you run out, and you never came back in."

I'm thinking she must not have seen Nick or anything since she didn't mention it. For that matter I don't feel like explaining the events of last night and reliving it yet, so I respond, "I saw Damon come through the door, and last second, we both decided to steal each other for the night. I'm sorry we didn't stay." Normally she'd make a bigger stink, but because I mention Damon, all seems to be forgiven. Well, that was easy.

After checking the rest of my messages, I head to the store to grab fresh ingredients for tonight's dinner. So many options run through my mind, but I decide to not go too big and keep it simple with tacos. Everyone loves tacos. After putting the groceries away and organizing the dinner ingredients on the counter for later, I pour myself a glass of wine and relax for a bit on the couch. Or at least I try to. My nerves won't let the alcohol do its thing, so I end up cleaning the entire apartment, even though I had just cleaned it a couple of days prior.

Damon calls me this time, letting me know he's here. He probably figures that hearing knocks on the door may make me nervous after all I went through with Nick, not that I expect him to come back anytime soon. I quickly finish up setting out the toppings for the tacos before letting him in. I expected this to be a more serious visit, but I didn't expect to see him not smiling at all. Instead, his face looks exactly as it did when he was lying in my bed, zoned in on my ceiling. He looks like he has a lot on his mind, and I mean a lot. I make him two tacos and bring it to the kitchen table. I go ahead and make mine as well before grabbing the rest of the wine from earlier; we're going to need this.

Before I take my first bite, I look at him and ask, "What's on your mind?"

"Let's wait until after we finish eating," he suggests.

"OK," I say with a little more worry than before.

Once we finish eating, we head over to the couch with our glasses of wine but not before I top mine off. Leaving me in suspense, he takes a deep breath. What could it possibly be? Then he puts his glass down on the ottoman tray, so I take in a big gulp and do the same. He stops looking at me while he takes another deep breath. He's looking at his hands in his lap that are pressed fingertips to fingertips as his mouth finally opens. He exhales and says, "I'm reenlisting."

I involuntarily blink fast a couple of times before shouting from the shock, "You're...you're what?"

He nods before calmly continuing, "For three years."

"When?" I ask, still trying to get my voice back down to its normal volume.

"The end of summer. I'll be here a few more weeks," he answers.

There is no way I'm hearing him correctly. I ask, "Why? Why now?"

He responds, "It's not something I decided suddenly, Delilah. I've been speaking with recruiters and thinking about it since before my last term ended. You were the only thing making me want to put it off."

"What's changed?" I demand. "Did I do something?"

Reaching for my hands, he says sympathetically, trying to calm me down, "No, you did absolutely nothing. I don't expect you to understand, but it's something I feel I need to do."

I look at our hands as I quietly ask, "How could you just leave? Leave me? I thought I was important."

"You are. I promise you are. I will come back," he says before trying to find my eyes with his, but I kept on looking down at our hands.

"How can you promise that?" I ask calmly.

"Look at me. I promise I'll come back for you," he affirms while reaching out to touch my cheek.

Unintentionally leaving him in suspense for almost one full minute while I think, I turn my chin away from him and somehow find the words I thought I'd never say. "I don't want to speak to you again." I slowly pull my hands away from his, laying them in my lap.

Looking defeated, he lowers his voice to its softest level. "Delilah, I...lo—"

Before he can finish, I interrupt him, leaving his words unspoken, "I don't want to hear any more. You're leaving, and that's that. There's nothing else I need to know. Please leave me alone."

He slowly nods in agreement before saying in a low voice, "You are the last person I ever wanted to hurt." Damon can tell I'm exhausted with this conversation along with him, so he takes his leave. I finally look up in time to watch him close the front door behind him.

I get up to lock the dead bolt before turning to lean against the wall for a while, still digesting our conversation. The rest of the night, I am reliving all the interactions we have ever had, trying to convince myself that I'm OK with all this. However, there's nothing I can tell myself to make this OK, not in the slightest. I'm so depressed that I end up lying in bed and not getting up until morning. The next couple of days, I am still in a slump while I try to come to terms with everything.

He waits a few days before messaging me, "Delilah, can we talk? I don't want to end things this way." I read his message several times before deciding to ignore it. There is nothing more we need to talk about.

Two weeks pass, and I have hardly felt motivated to leave my apartment. My phone, for the most part, has been silent. Emma will reach out to me every now and then to have a girls' day, but Damon hasn't messaged me since the last time he asked to speak. I'd be lying if I say I haven't picked up my phone multiple times, wanting to reach out to him. I always end up stopping myself because what is the point? He's leaving, and there is nothing I can possibly do to keep that from happening. He has already signed himself over.

Saturday arrives, and I receive a call from Emma asking if I'm going to karaoke tonight. I haven't been there since having the incident with Nick, which I'd still rather not tell her so I can avoid reliving it for a while longer if possible. I definitely haven't told her much about Damon, especially our last interaction. I'm not sure if he's talked about me to her, but I can only assume he has. The life is still being squeezed out of my heart, so I'd rather not see him if he's there. I don't even want to ask if he will be. I keep it simple and tell her I have a paper I'm behind on that's due on Monday, which is the truth.

Before she ends the call, she says, "Oh! While I have you, you're still coming to our annual end-of-summer beach trip in two weeks, right?"

"Eh…uh…yes," I reply. I always look forward to this trip. We usually go for a long weekend. Listening to the sounds of the waves and feeling the warmth of the sand under my feet sound like the perfect recipe for feeling refreshed and getting my mind off—what's his name? This time I probably should have asked if Damon is going to be there, but if I did, then she would surely know something has recently happened between us. That's if she's not aware already. Besides, even if he is, it won't change my mind on going. I am not missing this trip.

Another two weeks came and went, and Emma is outside my apartment, obnoxiously beeping her horn with music blaring, and shouts, "Get that peachy ass in the car! It's time to head to the beach!"

Beyond ecstatic, I run out to her jeep, throwing my luggage inside. Wherever they tumble to land is just fine with me. Then I run up to the front passenger door and get in before saying, "Let's not come back this time!" laughing but only half-joking.

SIX

As Emma and I near the coast, we see glimpses of the sparkling ocean around the hills and through the trees. We drive closer to the hotel, and I can see the powerful white waves breaking on the shoreline. We always have a place right on the beach for the ultimate experience. Being able to wake up early in the morning with the ocean as the first thing I see and hear while enjoying hot coffee is always the best start. If I wake up early enough, I can catch the undisturbed waters looking so pristine as if they were glass. Every so often dolphins can be seen breaching down the coast.

We get to the front door of the hotel to check in, and the very first thing I do after getting out from the jeep is fill my lungs with the salty ocean air, the same smell that greets us every time, bringing with it memories of our times here before. It's almost like we never left.

After checking in, a bellhop throws all our belongings onto a luggage cart and escorts us to our room located on the bottom floor. It has the quickest access to the water, which is why Emma requests it every time we come. I can map out every crack in the travertine floor by now. It holds two separate bedrooms with their own bathroom, which is super convenient for when either of us wants to retreat to recharge.

We enter the hotel room before separating into our private rooms to put our luggage down. I am still putting my clothes away in the drawer when Emma decides to kick things off by blaring Beach Boys. She comes running in my room already dressed in her bikini, cover-up, and probably the biggest hat I've ever seen. "Why are you just standing there?" she screeches.

Closing the drawer, I start, "I'm putting my—"

But she interrupts, "It doesn't even matter. All I know is you are doing the complete opposite of what we came here for. Put on your damn bikini!" She runs out my door in overwhelming excitement.

Absorbing that sudden burst of energy while sitting on my bed, I shake my head, laughing. I already see how this trip is going to go. Three minutes later I am dressed and head out to the common area, where she is lying on the couch with her leg up the back side. She stops looking at her phone to look at me. "About time!" she scolds.

I smile as I roll my eyes. "You're the one still lying on the couch! Let's go!" I lightheartedly snap back.

She pops up off the couch and sprints out the back door toward the beach. "Good thing I am here to remember to grab the sunscreen," I joke to myself as I grab it off the table before walking after her.

Eventually, I spot her on the sand. It's not too hard because she literally has the brightest pink tent out there, not to mention it is huge. I walk up to hand off the sunscreen as she looks at me. "Finally, you made it!" she says impatiently.

I laugh some more and grab us a couple of drinks from the cooler before laying my towel next to hers. She opens her book to read while I close my eyes. I have my hands slightly hanging off my towel, twirling my fingers through the sand, feeling every grain that falls between them. The sun is perfect, not too hot, yet I can still feel my body filling with its warmth. The roars of the waves start entering my thoughts before devouring my mind. And just like that, all of life's worries melt away.

We are here for another couple of hours before the sun lowers. Slowly, we pack up and head back to the room. We both take showers to wash all the sand off before discussing dinner. There is this new restaurant walking distance from the hotel along the beach with reverse happy hour and an open patio, so we decide to head over to check it out.

We are shown to our table with a server following right behind us to grab our first drink order. I don't even have time to look at the drink menu, not that it matters. I usually get one of three things anyway depending on my mood. Today feels like a mojito. He brings the drinks to our table in no time at all. As we sip them down, we watch all the action in the water from surfers to kids building sandcastles.

We are both about finished with our cocktails when the server comes to our table and asks if we would each like another round. "Oh, I'll have one!" Emma says. She is currently working on her second while I'm still finishing up my first. I've never been a huge drinker. But then the server looks at me for my answer.

"Sure!" I say. "I'm on vacation. Why not?"

He says, "Coming right up!" before heading back to his computer to ring the order in.

A few minutes later, my drink arrives. I am roughly half-way through it when I feel a change in my head. Emma and I stay at the restaurant a while longer, having such an incredible time, before stumbling out while linking arms for stability as we walk down the boardwalk back to our hotel for the night.

The next day the ocean wakes me up just in time to catch the dolphins breaching across our window. I sip on my freshly brewed coffee, thinking about the first thing Emma and I are going to do once we set up camp at the beach. There is already a good amount of people migrating to the sand before Emma wakes up.

Watching her emerge out of her room looking like a hot mess, I can't help but burst out laughing while offering to pour her a cup of coffee. She takes her first sip before I decide to give her a hard time. "About time you're up." I tease. "You are doing the complete opposite of what we came here for."

She looks at me unamused and takes another sip before asking, "How are you all chipper this morning?" She holds her head. "I feel like hell."

I laugh again as I say, "You just need the hair of the dog is all. Drink your coffee, get dressed, and let's head to the beach to fix that." I'm actually surprised I don't have a hangover. Having only one drink has the potential of throwing me over the edge, but in any case, I am not going to question a good thing.

She quickly drinks her coffee as if it were her first drink after running a marathon. While she gets ready, I pack up everything we could possibly need for an entire day at the beach. She appears from her room once again, but this time she looks like a totally different person. "I knew my Emma was in there somewhere," I joke.

"Ugh…let's just go. I want to lie on my towel and not move all day," she moans.

I laugh and say, "OK," before tossing her a beer. "Sip on that, and let's do this."

We set up camp at the beach. Then Emma sits down under her bright pink tent, finishing her hair of the dog. Meanwhile, I take a long walk down to the pier at the other end to warm up for the day ahead. By the time I am almost back to Emma, I can see her standing up. She is looking a million times better, 100 percent back to her normal self. I see her grab the Frisbee before standing to face me. I am almost back to our setup when she walks out toward the wet sand, so I detour and head in the same direction.

There are hardly any people this close to the water at the moment, so we take advantage of a wide area to throw and run. Emma is the first to toss the Frisbee. Her abilities are admirable. She can throw it so smoothly and strongly that even the opposing wind is unable to influence its direction. On the other hand, if I try to throw into the wind, the Frisbee will end up being swayed and usually comes back toward me like a boomerang. For that reason I always throw toward the direction where the wind is blowing and leave the more challenging way to Emma. We throw the Frisbee back and forth a few dozen more times before heading back to the cooler for some refreshments.

I figure Emma may want to lie down for a bit to recharge, so I sit down on my warm towel that's been baking in the sun. I look over to her, expecting her to follow my lead, but she instead bends over and grabs the ropes to our kayaks before holding them in the air. "Are you getting in on this or what?" she insists.

"This is what I came here for," I reply. "You just try to keep up."

I take the ropes to my kayak from her hand and run toward the waves, with it dragging in the sand behind me. I paddle out and almost get capsized by the last wave before hitting the calm zone. The wave came at me from a different angle from the others, so I quickly had to adjust the nose of my kayak in a direction more in my favor. Once we are both past the waves, we paddle even farther until all the noise from the waves and shore disappear. This is peace. Emma and I sit quietly, letting the water make our kayaks drift a little bit as we listen to all the noises that still remain. We hear a couple of splashes from fish jumping and short songs that the wind is singing. At one point a seagull flies by, granting us with a few squawks. We stay out here for a couple of hours longer before paddling back to shore.

When we coast back up to the shoreline, the sun is setting. We head back to our spot in the sand to pack up. As we get closer, I see a familiar face walking toward us, coming into focus. It's Damon, and he looks like he is walking our way from the direction of the hotel. Suddenly, here comes that hangover I didn't wake up with earlier.

He first hugs Emma before looking at me to probably get a feel of what I may be thinking. Out of the corner of my eye, I can see him waiting for me to look back at him, but I continue to look down at my towel as I roll it up. I also make sure to leave my facial expressions unreadable to the best of my ability. To be honest it's not too hard to do because I'm not sure exactly how I feel about him being here. I have planned on resenting him forever, but seeing him now, am I happy he is here?

He decides to speak up with much anticipation. "Hi, Delilah."

I want to keep things as neutral as possible without spoiling anyone's time. So I respond with "hi" and nothing else before looking back toward the sun, which is currently melting into the ocean about halfway.

He looks at Emma and asks if he can help bring everything back to our room. Of course, she agrees with zero hesitation. As I stand, gathering my stuff, I can overhear their conversation. "Thanks for inviting me," he tells her.

"Of course! It wouldn't have been complete without you. Where did you book your room?" she asks.

He points in the direction of our hotel and says, "Bottom floor, room 100."

Emma then gets excited and replies, "That's only three doors down from ours! Perfect."

"Not perfect," I think. As I overhear this, I realize that she has absolutely no idea about what's been going on between Damon and me, and I will not be the one to spark some drama on this trip. Plus, I came here to relax, and I'm not letting him get in the way of that. With his back turned to me, I watch him pick up most of our items and walk with Emma to our room while I keep a few feet behind.

Almost to the sliding glass door, the two of them are finalizing dinner plans as I choose to remain silent. Emma mentions where we went last night. "Delilah and I went to this cool spot yesterday. You have to come with to check it out." She looks at me for confirmation. "Right, Delilah? Wasn't it awesome?"

Not too keen on him going but also not wanting to be the Debbie Downer, I start, "Eh…yeah, the place was really cool." I say nothing more.

"Then it's settled!" exclaims Emma. "We will all get ready in our rooms and then meet back at ours after."

"See you both in a bit," he says as he puts down our things, leaving our hotel room to head to his but not without glancing at me one more time.

I again pretend not to notice as I try to look as busy as possible. I don't want to feel obligated to interact with him. I'd prefer to avoid any and all eye contact. After all, I know that the second his eyes catch mine, I'll be caught helpless.

Roughly an hour later, Damon is knocking on the door to our hotel room to escort us to dinner. We are showing him the way after all. The place has the same outgoing vibe as the night before. We are shown to our table on the patio before taking our seat. There is a different server this time on her way to take our order.

"What will it be?" the server asks.

Damon looks at me and asks, "What can I order for you to drink?"

I bypass him to answer her, "I will have a dry martini, please." I need something strong.

Damon shrugs it off and then gives his order along with Emma's to the server before she leaves. I'm watching the waves hit the shore as I feel his eyes on me. I can tell he is searching for words to say as much as I can tell he is scared of me not responding to them. The few questions he is brave enough to ask only really warrant one-word answers, so that's what I decide to give him. I could say more, but again, what's the point? Emma must be tuning in on Damon and me by now, but she decides to keep quiet, another admirable trait about her. She knows when to keep her comments to herself.

We are all feeling good and buzzy when the time comes to leave the restaurant. As we head back, Emma brings up to Damon another potential trip come winter. It doesn't take me long to realize that Damon has yet to mention anything to Emma about going away. He takes a few more steps while keeping his focus on the boardwalk in front of him. Then I hear him tell her he won't be here. I walk and stay a few feet ahead so I can let them talk.

"What do you mean you won't be here?" she asks.

He comes right out and says, "I decided to reenlist. I thought I told you."

"What?" she reactively shouts.

I'm thankful someone else is having this type of reaction. We just make it back to our room, and I slide the room key across the lock to open the door before walking inside. I hold the door open for Emma, but before she walks in, she looks at Damon and demands, "Come inside! We're not done talking yet."

This is awkward. I keep quiet for a minute, deciding what I'm going to do. A few minutes after we all gather in the common area, I grab water off the counter and tell both of them I'm heading to bed. It is still a bit early for that, but I don't want to be around him any more than I have to, especially for this conversation. Emma bids me good night, and I tell her the same. Then Damon chimes in, bidding me good night, only I leave him unanswered before closing the door to my room.

SEVEN

I brush my teeth before putting on my sweats and comfy shirt. Pulling my bedsheets back, I get in the bed and grab my phone. It's been a couple of days since I have looked in on social media, so I figure that's where I should start. As I click through everything and catch up, it doesn't take too long before a message comes through.

"You could be a little more respectful," I read. It's from Damon.

I am stuck, rereading it several times, not being able to help myself. I respond, "I'm giving you all the respect I believe you deserve from me." I know it's harsh and out of character, but I'm hurting, and I want him to hurt. Then I put my phone on silent before laying it face down on the hotel's bedside table.

While I'm trying to fall asleep, I still hear him and Emma chatting up a storm at the table in the common area. He is telling her all the details about his military contract. I also hear him mention my name in the conversation, but I can hardly make out any part of that. To be honest I'm trying to muffle it all by squashing my head in between the pillow, folding it around my ears. Unfortunately, it's only a sad attempt because I can still hear enough to put together the rest of what he is saying. I am obviously not getting to sleep, and the last thing I want to do is lie here and be forced to listen to it. So I put on my flip-flops and head out the back door toward the beach, not saying a word to either one. Maybe Damon will get the hint and head back to his hotel room.

Only a few feet out of the hotel I find a spot to sit on the beach. I lean back on my hands, sliding them deeper into the cool sand while looking up at the vivid stars. They are crystal clear and look to be in clusters by the millions. Stars like these don't happen in the city, especially in Phoenix. There is way too much light pollution. My eyes shift from looking through the sky to looking out into the ocean. The tide is coming in. I patiently sit and watch as my mind again starts to feel at ease.

I am out here for quite some time, and it's getting colder by the minute. If I wasn't in such a hurry to get out of there, I would have grabbed a sweater. I refuse to go back in until I'm positive that Damon's gone, so I hug my knees into my chest and stubbornly wait it out.

Several minutes later I hear a familiar voice behind me. I look behind my shoulder to see Damon asking the hotel security guard, who patrols the grounds at night, if he has seen me. So he will not cause a scene, I call out his name, luring him over to where I'm sitting. He walks over and continues to stand with the most serious look on his face before speaking. "What are you doing out here by your-self?" he lectures.

He has no right to ask me this or to be concerned. Watching the waves creep even closer, still avoiding all pos-sible eye contact with him, I answer back, "It was the only way to get away from you."

He sighs. "Come back inside," he says, while reaching his hand out to help me stand up.

I look at his hand for a brief moment before looking back toward the tide. "I'm fine," I say firmly.

"Tell me what I can do," he desperately insists.

Knowing it won't make a difference, I look at him as I vent my feelings about him leaving one last time. He doesn't even try to stick up for himself. Instead, he just lets me tear into him before I turn my focus back to the ocean.

Frustrated, he sits down next to me for a moment in silence. Then he starts telling me random stories about him growing up. I act like I'm not interested, but I am truly soaking up every word. I laugh as I let my guard down. He pauses his storytelling to look at me with a smile. I love his smile. I'm unable to look away from him any longer. Our eyes finally meet and intensely lock. What I was afraid of happening is happening: I demolish the wall that was built solely for Damon.

After finishing his last story, he stands up once again, reaching his hand out for mine. This time I decide to give in and reach my hand back to his. He grabs it tight and pulls me to my feet. We walk side by side toward the waves. As we approach, jokes are flying between the two of us. I see him stop walking, but I continue on a few feet closer to the water. Then I feel a cold splash hit the back of my legs. I turn around and see his foot almost back on the ground after kicking water at me.

"Oh, that's it!" I shout while charging at him.

He catches me just as we collide, tackling me to the ground. A wave has freshly retreated, so we are getting muddier than anything as we continue to wrestle. I roll him over so his back is against the sand while I lie on top, pinning him down. We are mesmerized with each other when a surprise wave comes up, soaking both of us head to toe, ending our match with the ocean as the only winner. He quickly stands to his feet, lifting me out of the water before bringing me in close as we walk back to the hotel. We are both cold, wet, and full of mud, but it makes the night even better. However, I could use a hot shower.

When we get back inside, Emma is already asleep in her room with the door closed. Damon invites himself into our hotel room before heading back to his. All I can think about is that shower. I am so cold that I don't care about anything else, so I lock the back door before running to my room.

I'm starting to get some dry clothes out of my drawer when I notice him follow me inside. He walks right past me and turns on the shower in the bathroom, purposely leaving the door wide open. My eyes grow wide as I stand still, unable to do anything but face his direction. I watch him take off his clothes while the bathroom fills with dense steam. His clothes are so wet that they are basically sticking to him. All the friction forces him to pull off his shirt extremely slow as my jaw begins to slightly drop. At least I hope it's slight. Then he goes after his pants, and the same thing happens. He is so dedicated with his unintentional striptease.

As he enters the shower, I'm still not able to look away. I am trying as hard as I can, but my eyes won't budge. I'm watching him run his hand down his neck with soap before he catches my stare and stops, leaving his hand in place. I'm so caught, yet I suddenly don't care. We both look at each other, and I become entranced. His eyes are calling me closer. How are they able to have this much power over me?

I can't help but walk into the shower with him. I am so under his spell that I don't even bother taking my clothes off. The moment I step inside, he pulls me in with intention and begins kissing me harder than ever as he is impatiently tearing at my clothes. He then pushes me up against the tile wall and goes down to both knees. Gently spreading my legs open, he starts showing me everything his tongue can do. And oh my gosh, I tremble almost instantly. He continues to go a moment longer while I fall weak at my knees, my back sliding down the wall toward the floor, forcing him to hold me up. Then he stands to his feet, lifting me and carrying me out of the shower to my bed.

Before laying me on top of the sheets, he continues kissing me. His tongue can do anything. Then he throws me down to the bed before climbing on top. He kisses me a little longer while he has his fingers between my legs, twirling inside me. Then he turns me over to my side, spooning me from behind. He enters himself into me an inch at a time before pulling out, making me crave for a full and deep thrust. He eventually gives me just what I'm hoping for, and I find myself clenching the sheets in front of me as I bury my moan into them. He thrusts hard a few more times before pulling out and finishing. Grabbing a towel, he wipes up the mess before spooning with me again as we fall asleep.

In the morning I can hear Emma getting up. Normally she's the one who sleeps in so when she comes out of her room and doesn't see me having coffee, she gets a little worried. I hear her footsteps running through the common area toward my door shortly before she bursts in. I grab the sheets and hold on tight as she tugs on them to try to get me out of bed. Damon is ducking underneath, so she doesn't realize he is in here with me. But then she tears at the sheets from the bottom of the bed, lifting a corner, exposing his legs. She immediately starts jumping up and down while blushing. Then she smiles very big before walking backward toward the door, shutting it behind her. Damon and I look at each other and laugh before rolling out of bed to find some clothes. His are all still soaked from the night before, so he leaves them to dry in the bathroom and runs back to his room in nothing but his briefs.

I head out to the common area and see Emma sipping from her coffee mug on the sofa while looking at me with another huge grin. I look at her, silently smiling, and we end up almost telepathically having an agreement to not mention anything about what she saw only a few minutes ago. So I sit down beside her with some coffee of my own as I replay the entire night in my head. I'm lost in the clouds, thinking about him, when I remember that he's leaving in just a few short weeks. What am I doing?

While finishing my coffee, I decide I won't give him the silent treatment again, but I'm also not going to lead him on any further. After all, my feelings about him leaving still haven't changed.

Once Emma and I are dressed, she calls Damon to let him know we are about to head down to the beach. In no time at all, he is at our door, ready to escort us. As we leave our hotel room, I feel his hand trying to grab mine, but I pull away and smile. He looks at me confused, so I give him another smile before continuing our walk.

He walks a bit closer to me and asks, "Is everything OK?"

"Yes, fine," I reply. "It's just that nothing has changed. You're still leaving."

He looks down. "I want to enjoy the time I have left with you."

"It's just prolonging the inevitable. I'm still going to be here, picking up the pieces after you leave," I say.

"I'm going to be a wreck too, Delilah," he says.

"At least you had a choice in the matter," I strike before going silent.

After we set up the area at the sand, I decide I want to go for a walk by myself. So I let them know I'll be back in a bit. "Where are you headed?" Emma asks.

"Um, I'm just going up to the bar on the boardwalk to grab a cocktail," I reply.

"Oooh!" she says. "That sounds wonderful! We'll come too." Then she links my arm with hers as she tries to force a skip in the sand. Damon follows closely behind.

When we arrive to the outside bar, we decide to take a seat at a table. I change my mind and go for a Dos XX instead of a cocktail. Emma and Damon follow my lead. As we all sit here enjoying our drinks and talking, another beer is set in front of me. Before the bartender can walk off to head back behind the bar, I grab his attention. "Pardon me, but I did not order this," I tell him.

He says, "This is from him," as he points to a man sitting by himself at the bar. Damon is obviously right next to me, watching all this. I don't know what else to do other than put my new drink up in the air, thanking the man at the bar for sending it over, even though an order of tacos would have been better. Then I put my drink down, glancing over to Damon, before noticing the gentleman at the bar getting up from his seat. I see him coming to our table, and not knowing what's about to happen, I look at Damon. Damon is wearing the best poker face I've ever seen. I can't tell at all what he is thinking. I can only imagine he's not happy. The guy gets to our table, pulls out a chair, and sits himself right between Damon and me, incredibly bold if I say so myself. My heart is racing. What in the world is happening right now?

"Hi, what's your name?" the stranger asks.

"Delilah," I answer before looking down at my hands resting on the table. I don't ask for his name.

"Where are you from?" he then asks.

I keep my answer very vague and say, "Phoenix." Again, I don't ask about him back. I am hoping he gets the hint and leaves because I am officially feeling incredibly awkward. I glance at Damon, who is completely focused on this guy who is literally coming between us. His facial expression still hasn't changed to anything more than unreadable.

"Would you like to go for a walk?" the stranger asks.

I end the conversation by saying, "Eh...I actually just got done walking, and I'm taking a break. Maybe I can catch you later. Thank you for the drink."

He finally gets the hint, stands up without pushing the chair in, and leaves. We all look at one another as Emma and I talk about what has just happened. Damon still doesn't say a word and keeps his unfazed facial expression. I try to bite my tongue but end up saying, "Now there's a man who knows what he wants." Emma folds her lips in and looks away from the table while Damon gives me a sharp and memorable stare.

We tab out before heading back to the beach for a bit longer. Upon arriving to our site, Damon tells us he'll be back in a bit as he walks off toward the pier. I guess I struck a nerve. That is perfectly fine as it leaves Emma and me some time to talk about what we are doing tonight.

She mentions a local club down the block that has dancing and live music almost every night. We've been there before on one of our past trips, but I forgot about it, which is shocking because I remember it being a highlight. I tell her that sounds perfect. "It does, doesn't it?" Emma says. "Once Damon gets back, I'll let him know the plans."

"OK!" I say, pretending to be excited.

I stare toward the pier to watch for Damon so that once he is heading back this way, I can leave for the hotel room and avoid him, while I'm able to anyway. A long while later, I can make out his silhouette in the distance. He is still so far away that I can't entirely tell to which direction he is walking. Just to be safe, I'll head back to the room now. This way I can fully compose myself for this evening's festivities.

I stand up, brushing the sand from under my thighs before grabbing as many beach supplies as I can. Hopefully, this leaves Damon with less excuses to stop by on his way back to his room. "I'll catch you back at the room, Emma," I say before slinging my bag over my shoulder.

"OK, I'll wait here for Damon. See you shortly," she replies.

When I get back to the room, I walk toward the bathroom, taking out my hair tie, allowing my wound-up bun to untangle as it falls down to my waist. Then I take off my clothes one piece at a time, leaving a trail on the floor leading to the shower. As I turn on the water, I look at the shower wall and get flashbacks of Damon and me from the night before. I shake it out of my head before stepping in. I can feel the leftover sand tickling down my skin and between my toes before going down the drain. At one moment my mind is racing, but now letting this shower massage my scalp, I find it almost blank.

Once I step out of the shower and walk back to the bedroom, I hear Emma come in through the back door. I pause for a moment to listen for voices, but I don't hear any, which must mean Damon is back in his room. Taking a deep breath, I look at my clothes, deciding what to wear tonight. There's going to be dancing, so of course, a dress is the only thing that seems fitting enough. I have brought a couple on the trip and hung them in the closet. I pull out the exact one I am thinking of. It is white and mid-length. It hugs all my curves perfectly, and the sleeves have rope ties, giving it a perfect beach vibe. I walk out of my room to the common area once I'm ready to wait for Emma.

She hears me opening a can of beer and shouts, "I'll be out in one minute!" before adding, "Oh! And Damon messaged me saying he's running behind and will meet us there."

I shout back, "Sounds good to me!"

As soon as she's ready, she comes out of her room. I see her wearing the tightest pair of skinny jeans and a white crop top complete with white Converse. She actually pulls that look off incredibly well, but I tease, "How are you going to dance in that?"

"You just worry about keeping up," she teases back.

I laugh and say, "You're the one who's going to be late. I'm already halfway to the jeep," as I bolt out the front door. She takes a moment before sprinting after me, nearly catching up. I forgot she did track all through high school. With both of us screaming from excitement as we approach the vehicle, I tag both my hands on the jeep's door first. Then I bend over to catch my breath, while she is not even fazed. I don't think her heart rate went up in the slightest; meanwhile, I'm over here gasping for air before we get in and buckle up.

Emma and I arrive to the parking lot, and the moment we get out of the car, we hear the band blasting from inside. "Oooh," I say, "this guarantees a good time!" We are practically running through the parking lot toward the entrance. Once we get inside, we hear the band playing a song by George Strait. Without hesitation we make our way to the dance floor.

Several songs later we are both dying of thirst. So I scope out the place for the bar since I don't quite remember where it is. "There's a bar outside on the patio!" Emma shouts in my ear because it is insanely loud in here.

"Let's do it!" I shout back as we hold hands, with her leading the way through the crowd toward the back patio.

We grab a couple of stools that are cemented in place at the bar and spin to face each other as we wait for the bartender to come around. The music is blaring just as loud out here. Too focused on trying to hear our conversation while jumping from one topic to the other, I haven't noticed if the bartender has stopped by or not. I lean in a little closer to Emma's mouth, trying to hear her better, when suddenly I feel someone grinding on me from behind.

I turn around and see this stranger standing behind my barstool, looking like he is ordering a drink. He is thin and wearing loose and worn-out-looking clothes. His hair is all gray and overgrown along with his facial hair. Needless to say, the guy looks rough and not far from being homeless. I brush it off, thinking it must have been a mistake while he was trying to grab the bartender's attention or something. Turning back toward Emma to continue our conversation, I forget all about the incident. We get to talking for roughly two minutes until, suddenly, it happens again, even harder. I swear I can feel his hands lightly caressing my hips as well. I jolt out of the chair with a scream, jumping into Emma's lap.

Damon, of course, walks up just in time to catch the entire thing and once again runs to my rescue without me asking. He hurries to stand between me and the man, facing him. He has me standing behind him slightly off to the side so he can make sure I'm safe in his view as he sizes the creep up. Damon is bigger by a long shot in every way. He stays calm while in a broad stance, holding one hand over the other in front of his waist while telling the guy to back away. I step around so I am able to fully view Damon from the side, and he looks like he has an animal inside him waiting to be released if the man makes the wrong move. Suddenly, the creep waves both of his hands up by his head, signaling a surrender.

Once I get a good enough idea of what the end result will be, I head back inside to the dance floor, away from Damon, without saying anything. Emma stays outside with him for a bit before meeting me back inside for a few more dances. Damon hasn't tried to come and talk to me at all tonight since scaring off the guy on the patio. I don't even see him around as I glance through the crowd while dancing.

When it's time to head out, Emma says she needs to use the restroom first, so I tell her I'll be outside, warming up the jeep since it's cold again tonight. I suspect Damon has kept a watchful eye on me all night because I'm not too far out in the parking lot when he comes running up behind me. "Delilah!" he shouts as he gets closer.

I continue walking while he quickens his pace to catch up, "Can we please talk? I hate this. I hate that you won't talk to me."

Just as he catches up to me, I make it to the car and turn on the engine before stepping out. "What, Damon? What can you possibly say?"

He stammers, trying to find something to say that I may find acceptable. While he's doing that, Emma almost catches up to us. I am so focused on his rambling as he is desperately trying to find the words to make all this OK that I don't even notice Emma stopping to listen in on us for a moment. She must have heard enough because she gets into the jeep and drives off without me, leaving me stranded with him. Damon and I both pause while we watch her exit the parking lot before looking at each other again. That was a dirty play, good on her part but dirty.

What she just did spares Damon from having to answer my question. He instead says, "Here, I'll take you back to your room."

Unsure of my answer, I respond, "No thank you. I can walk."

He quickly says, "But it's late, and it must be at least over five miles!"

"What's your point? Think I can't do it?" I question him.

He must be getting so annoyed, but he keeps his patience. "Please let me take you back. We don't have to talk. I promise I won't say a word," he pleads.

"Not one word," I demand as he opens the passenger door for me to get in. He makes it so hard to be mad at him.

The silence in the truck only lasts about halfway through the drive as he can no longer contain himself. "Are you cold?" he asks while reaching for the air controls.

"Not one word," I repeat. "And I'm fine, thank you."

Once we're back to the hotel, he gets out first to come around and open my door. This time I beat him to it and open the door myself. He stops in place and smiles slightly while I lead the way to my room. He drops me off at the front door without saying a word. I slide my room key over the lock to walk inside but not before turning to face him and saying, "Good night."

He looks up at me and smiles. "Good night," he happily responds before walking to his room.

Knowing we are all headed back home in the morning, I cannot sleep. I'm up extra early before sunrise and head to the beach by myself, sipping on my hot coffee. I am sucking it down because it is still chilly out, and I want all this hotness in my belly. I watch the tide still receding as I listen to the loud roar of the waves, greeting me "good morning." I'm out here for about an hour longer before heading back inside.

Damon is in our room with his bags packed, ready to get on the road. Emma, I'm sure, hasn't even begun packing yet, so we'll be behind by a couple of hours, I imagine. He stops and looks at me for a moment in silence before deciding to speak. "I know you probably won't want to see me when we get back, so I wanted to be sure to tell you goodbye now," he regretfully says.

My heart stops abruptly; he's right. Why would I have to see him? I pause and stand still as he hesitantly walks in my direction. I don't move or say anything, which gives him the courage to wrap his arms around me. He leans in, giving me the longest hug we have ever shared, and he's hugged me in the past for some pretty good lengths of time.

Once he releases me, he takes a step back and says, "Delilah, I…I've always lo—"

He's interrupted by Emma running out of her room. "Oh my gosh!" she screams in sadness. "I can't believe it's already time to leave!" She looks up into the heavens. "Please give me four more days. Just four!"

Damon steps away from me and toward Emma, letting her know he's heading off. She gives him a big hug, saying she'll see him when she gets home. After glancing at me one last time, he picks up his things and walks out the door. I watch him carefully, knowing that this moment will be imprinted in my memory forever.

EIGHT

Damon and I haven't seen each other since our beach vacation. Emma has invited me out to karaoke for the last couple of weeks, but I haven't gone. Part of it is because I don't want to run into Damon if he happens to be there. It will be even harder having to say goodbye to him for a third time. I don't think I'd have the strength to be able to do so if given the opportunity.

Another week passes before I get a call from Emma. She asks me to go for pedicures later this afternoon. I'm rarely capable of saying no to those, so she knows that's the best bait to use. I get dressed to leave my apartment after three weeks, with the exception of grabbing groceries at the store, that is.

When I arrive to the nail salon, she again has two chair basins filled up for us and ready to go. We sit down next to each other, placing our feet in the bubbles in silence for a moment before she speaks. She gets straight to it. "Did Damon stop by or call you this morning?"

With a questionable expression, I reply, "No. Is he OK?"

"Well," she begins, "he left this morning. I was hoping he'd try to reach out to you."

Soaking it all in for a moment, I reply, "I didn't give him a reason to. I already told him goodbye," before looking down at the suds swirling around my ankles.

She sits quietly for another moment before talking some more. "He asked me for advice."

My ears perk up. Advice? About me? To my knowledge he's never asked for advice from her about me. I have never talked to her about him. I turn to look at Emma without saying anything as she continues, "He sounded desperate while asking me what he can do to get you to speak to him again."

"What did you tell him?" I ask with piqued interest.

"Time," she says. "I told him time."

I smile at her. That is probably the best thing she could have told him. His words will only make me angry. I decide to go with my signature pink nail color before saying bye to her and heading back home to my apartment.

As I attempt to put the subject of Damon as far from my mind as possible, I focus on finishing up the rest of my course assignments since the class will be ending soon. For the next couple of weeks, I am pumping out paper after paper until there are no assignments left, finishing the class two weeks ahead of schedule. Now what am I going to use as a distraction?

I know what I'll do—Emma. I give her a call, and she is just getting done with her gardening and asks if I would like to go to yoga with her. I can't think of anything more perfect, so I get ready and meet her at the yoga studio she suggests. Today happens to be yin yoga, one of my favorites. The idea is to hold deep stretches long enough to make a person break if he or she doesn't choose to welcome the associated pain and use it as information. There's always a good mix of being challenged physically and mentally. We don't talk about Damon, not that we're allowed to talk once class begins anyway. It's actually quite refreshing since I'm still trying to forget about him, with little success, I might add. We head to brunch after a heated yoga session and talk of future adventures now that we'll be entering into cooler weather.

"You know what I've always been interested in doing more?" she asks.

"What is that?" I question back.

"I'd like to go hiking around the sights of Arizona. I've lived here my entire life and have barely explored it," she says.

"That actually sounds like a great idea. Do you have room for one more?" I ask.

"I wouldn't want to do it without you." she happily says.

"Let's go on the weekends after my graduation in a few weeks," I suggest.

"Deal," she says.

When it is time for me to put on my cap and gown to get ready to head to the auditorium for my diploma, I think of everyone who is not able to be here to share my accomplishment that I have worked endlessly for. My mom is still not quite strong enough to leave the house just yet. And never knowing my dad means he has zero idea I am even graduating, let alone exist. Luckily for me I have Emma; she has made it one of her life missions to attend every important event of mine as I do hers.

As I take my seat in the auditorium, I look at the stands. Knowing there is no way he can be here, I look up at Emma in hopes of seeing Damon sitting next to her. As I am imagining what his face would look like and what he'd be dressed in, I hear my name get called to come up on stage and receive my certificate. Even though it literally only takes five seconds to walk from one side of the stage to the other, while I'm up here, it feels like an hour of standing under the spotlight. The crowd cheers as they do for everyone, but I can especially hear Emma's voice above all the others.

After the graduation ceremony, Emma takes me out for some celebratory drinks, and we end up making a night of it before splitting a cab on the way back to our places. We have enjoyed ourselves so much that there is definitely no escaping a hangover for either of us this time.

I spend a few days recuperating and not doing too much. I'm actually able to fully relax because, for the first time in forever, I have zero obligation. Nothing is making my mind race or calling for my attention. After taking several days to reset my mind, I start mapping out plans and areas to go to with Emma.

We should hike a local known, popular mountain, Camelback. I've done parts of the hike when I was younger but really haven't gone near it as an adult. I call her up to share my idea, and she wants to go this very weekend. I have to dig out my old CamelBak backpack. There is no telling where that could be. I look through boxes I've set aside and kept unpacked. It's mostly stuff I don't use all that much. But I don't see it. There is one last spot it may be. I reach up to the top of my closet and pull on a strap, knocking down a mountain of bags. There it is, easy to notice with that reservoir tube sticking out. I pack it full of things we'll need and set it aside for the weekend.

Camelback Mountain is halfway between Emma's house and mine, so we drive separately to meet there. I see her pull into the parking lot shortly after my arrival. I'm already at the base of the mountain, sizing it up, as she closes the door to her jeep and walks over. "Well, let's get going!" I say with enthusiasm.

Emma looks up at the mountain before looking at me and says without hesitancy, "Let's show this mountain it has nothing on us."

After taking breaks in just about every shady patch we can find along the trail, we finally make it to the very top. We find a rock big enough for both of us to use as a seat. It's in a prime location as it is heavily shaded by two saguaros that just happen to be in the perfect spot to hide the sun. We stare off in the distance, sitting in silence, soaking it all in. Roughly an hour later, we make our way back down, with both of our feet sliding on loose gravel every now and then along the way.

As we walk back to our cars, exhausted, we throw out ideas for our next adventure. "You know what's always been on my list?" Emma asks rhetorically.

With a questioning expression, I reply, "No, tell me."

"Havasu Falls," she says. "That is definitely a bucket list item."

"Well then, we have to do it!" I tell her, full of excitement.

She shrieks. "Promise? That would be the greatest adventure ever."

I laugh and respond, "Promise! I'll look into it once we recover from this one."

The only thing I really know about it so far is that it's located on an Indian reservation. So we'll have to get a permit and schedule a date in advance to visit. I'll look more into it in the computer when I get home, after a well-deserved shower and nap, of course.

Once I wake up refreshed, I google all the details I can about Havasu Falls. While looking to reserve a campground and permit, I see that we can have access in as early as six months, so I book it without thinking twice. From what I've heard, sometimes it can take even longer to get a date scheduled, so I'm happy with it only being this long. After grabbing the rest of the details for the trip, I call Emma to let her know.

"Holy cow!" she exclaims. "That's amazing! I can't wait."

I tell her, "Get your mind right. It's a long hike down."

Hesitating, she asks, only half-joking, "Oh, that's fine. Do they have someone who can help bring down our gear?"

I laugh and say, "Oh, you mean donkeys!"

She pauses for a moment before saying, "Well, that's not what I'd call them, but—"

"Oh my gosh, Emma!" I interrupt. "Actual donkeys. Sometimes you make me scratch my head." I start laughing hysterically. Before hanging up, I list all the items to bring that the website suggests.

"Got it," she says before continuing, "Let's shop together for everything we'll need. Should we go grab all the items on the list the week before we leave?"

"Works for me. Let's go that Saturday. I'll come pick you up," I reply.

"Great. There's a camping store not too far down the street from the karaoke lounge. Maybe we can do karaoke after," she says.

"I like that," I reply before saying goodbye and ending the call.

NINE

For the next six months, Emma and I have been finding things to keep us preoccupied and to prepare us for our big Havasu Falls trip. We've been going to the Phoenix Rock Gym almost weekly and doing small local hikes every two weeks or so. So far, we have added South Mountain, Piestewa Peak, and Papago to the list. We have even ventured up to Sedona a couple of times to do some popular hikes there like West Fork, Cathedral Rock, and Devil's Bridge Trails. Every single hike offers its own kind of beauty as well as individual meditative responses. Sedona is well known for its energy-filled vortices located throughout. I'm not too sure of all the vortex locations, but I do know that if I see a tree trunk growing in a twist, it is said to be one. And I happened to see one while we were hiking Cathedral Rock. We couldn't resist sitting under its provided shade for a bit to see if we can tap into its energy. We were both unsuccessful, and it was probably because we were too eager to get to the top and then back down when it was time to get lunch.

We are finally a week out from the big trip we have been planning. Emma's way of saying "good morning" apparently is blowing up my phone as soon as the sun comes up so we can go over everything. I'm barely half-awake, so I tell her I'll give her a call later. After having my coffee, I get so busy doing other things that I end up not calling her until three o'clock.

"You forgot about me," she accuses.

"Well…yeah…but only for, like, a minute," I respond, hoping to get a laugh out of her.

"That's fine, I'm over it. Are you still picking me up?" she asks.

"I will be there at five." I reply.

"OK, I'll be ready!" She shrieks in excitement.

We arrive at the store and each grab a cart for the items on our list. After getting the first couple of items, we eventually find ourselves making our way up and down every aisle, throwing additional items into the cart. Emma finds a bright pink tennis ball and holds it up. "This will be perfect!" she exclaims.

"Now what on earth are you possibly going to need that for?" I ask.

She answers, "You never know. We could get bored or something."

Looking at her perplexed, I ask, "You're worried you might get bored in a place like Havasu Falls?"

Then I continue, "OK, throw it in."

"Yes!" she yips while practically jumping up and down.

"The little things," I say, laughing.

We continue checking the rest of the items off the list before heading to the cashier. I watch the cashier load our items into the plastic grocery bags to full capacity. If we didn't have a cart to carry the bags out, then I would have probably asked her to double-bag them. I can literally see corners of our items bulging out of the bag, testing its plasticity.

After loading our bags into the carts, we walk out to the parking lot to transfer them into my car. "Here, I'll take the carts to the rack," insists Emma.

"OK," I say as I continue, "I'll start the car."

"Deal," she says as she grabs hold of my cart while throwing her last couple of bags into the trunk.

As soon as I hear the engine turn, I look over our camp supply list again to make sure we got all our items while I wait for Emma to finish up. As my eyes reach the very bottom, I hear a sudden, loud boom, making me jump so high in my seat that my head practically hits the roof. I quickly look up in my rearview mirror for Emma, but I don't see her. All I see is a guy running away, so I open my door. Stepping out, I see the bright pink tennis ball on the ground, wedged under my front wheel. Thinking it must have rolled, I look up, expecting to find a mess of items on the ground that have probably fallen from a torn bag. Instead, I see Emma lying on the ground, holding her stomach, with a pile of blood slowly forming around her.

My heart sinks as Emma suddenly comes a thousand more times into focus. I run over to her before falling to my knees in the bloody puddle. She is losing a lot of blood. She has been shot, and the guy I saw running away must have been the shooter. Her purse is gone.

Without thinking, I do the only thing I know how to do, and that is apply pressure. I quickly grab a blanket we just bought in the store out of my trunk and push down hard at the entry point with one hand as I dial 911 with the other. Somehow I also find the ability to scream for help during all this. I am quickly surrounded by a crowd of people; not one person can actually offer any help.

The police along with the ambulance arrive just as Emma begins showing signs of going into shock. As the paramedic team rushes in, I take a few steps back, giving them room. They work on stabilizing Emma as much as possible before transporting her. An officer walks my way. My head is spinning so fast that it takes me a moment to realize that the man walking toward me is Officer Jones. Before saying anything, he stands by me and scopes out the entire parking lot, making sure it's safe. I watch his eyes as they track every person walking inside and outside the store as well as people getting in and out of their vehicles. He stands there without saying anything until the ambulance drives off with Emma, pulling my heart with it. He gives me another moment in my catatonic-like state before snapping me out of it.

He says, "A bystander gave us the shooter's description as well as the direction he was running to. We have units tracking him right now," hoping I find some comfort.

It's not comforting though. The only thing I care to know in this moment is if Emma will be OK, which no one is able to tell me. I don't know what to respond to him, so I stand there quietly, getting lost in all the chaos around me. I can tell he is thinking of something else to say when suddenly his police radio blows up. He makes sure I stay close to him as we walk toward his patrol car. Then he grabs his radio and asks them to repeat it.

The officer on the other end of the radio says, "He's dead. Suspect open fired at police officers, and we were forced to end the threat. No officers or further civilians hurt in isolated shooting."

Suddenly, I take a deep breath before bursting out crying. I am not even aware that I had momentarily stopped breathing. Officer Jones continues to stand next to me while the other officers take care of the paperwork and other details, finalizing everything. All the emergency vehicles clear out of the parking lot except for him. I'm still hardly able to move as I remain in complete disbelief. Even though I have literally lived through this event, it still doesn't seem possible. How could that have been real?

Officer Jones takes a step away before turning to face me. "You're in no condition to drive," he says. "I'll take you home, if that's OK."

Still in shock, all I can do is nod as I struggle to say, "Thank you."

He hands me a tissue from his glove box to wipe my tears away. Then he holds open the passenger side to his patrol car and has me get in. I'll just hail a taxi back here in the morning for my car, no big deal.

Once we get back to my apartment, he sees me safely to my door. Before turning the key in the lock, I turn to face him and ask, "How am I going to tell Emma's mom? I don't know what to say."

"The hospital will call her," he answers.

"No," I say, "she needs to hear it from me."

"I can stay here while you make the call if you like," he offers.

"Thank you, but you've done plenty already. I appreciate you seeing me home safe," I reply.

"I hope I'm not crossing the line," he says. "But I want to give you my phone number in case you may ever need anything."

"Oh...OK...thank you," I say while I hand him my phone for him to save it in.

He then hands it back to me, and I look at the screen before I question, "Blake?"

"Yes," he says, "please call me Blake and don't hesitate to reach out to me if you need anything at all." Again, the only words I'm able to come up with are "thank you." He walks back out to his car.

I go into the apartment, and the first thing I do is look at my phone to call Emma's mom. But as I look at her contact information, I hesitate. While trying to summon up the courage to continue, her name appears on my screen. She beat me to it. "Hello, Mrs. Ross," I say as calmly as possible. "I was just about to call you."

With her voice trembling, she says, "I've already heard. They have her stable and are running diagnostics currently. I'm calling to make sure you are OK."

I can't stop myself from breaking down, even though I know I should be the one holding Mrs. Ross together. After all, she's the one who has a daughter in the hospital, currently fighting for her life. Choking back tears, I tell her, "I'm so sorry, Mrs. Ross. I would have given anything to prevent it."

She cries with gratitude. "I know you would have, dear. I'm packing up my bag to head over to the hospital now. Try to get some rest and maybe come see her in the morning during visiting hours if you feel up to it. You both have been through a lot, so no pressure at all."

"I will be there," I say firmly before hanging up the phone.

Somehow I feel utterly exhausted yet fully wired at the same time. Maybe I'll be able to sleep after a shower. I go and turn the water on to the hottest setting before stepping in. Water always has this magical power of washing the day away and not just the accumulated dirt but the negative stress and energy as well. If only its magic was strong enough to wash away today. I can't do anything else but stand here for a while, not even reaching for the soap. I pay special attention to the water hitting the roots of my hair and trickling down, feeling the drops trail over my ankles before whirlpooling down the drain. The hot water feels so good that I'm getting goose bumps as I stand here, welcoming the feeling.

Twenty more minutes pass by before I think about stepping out and getting into bed. I quickly wash up with soap and rinse off. Finally, I turn off the water and grab my towel. I slip on the comfiest pajamas I can find and pull back my covers to get in. I then burrow myself in the bed before turning off the light. Unfortunately, I'm still unable to sleep. I can't stop thinking of Emma. What is she going through right now? Is she OK?

Hours pass, and I still lay here awake. I keep looking at the clock, but it has never moved slower. Emma's mom told me that the hospital doesn't open for visitors until ten in the morning, and it is only five o'clock. Staring at the clock, watching the minutes slowly pass by, I end up falling asleep sometime around six thirty. My alarm goes off at eight o'clock, giving me enough time to get ready. I still have to take a taxi back to my car. Once I pick that up, I'm going to grab some flowers and a triple espresso on the way to the hospital. We'll see how the caffeine handles one and a half hours of sleep.

The taxi driver drops me off to my car. The stores don't open for another hour, so when I step out and close the door, I am completely alone. There is no other car in sight after the taxi leaves. All of yesterday instantly hits me as my eyes roam the ground where Emma was lying. I get lost while envisioning her there. The breeze picks up and blows leaves across the bloodstains left behind. I feel myself going to a dark place before coming to.

I quickly walk to the driver's side door to get in. But as I go to sit down, I see Emma's bright pink tennis ball still wedged under my tire. I bend down to grab it and place it in the passenger seat to take with me before getting on my way. Next is a stop to the store for fresh white lilies, her favorite. And of course, I can't forget my extra strong latte on the way out.

I arrive to the hospital front desk, and a lady shows me the location of Emma's room using a floor map. Walking down the hallway, I am getting more anxious as I near her door. When I enter, I see Emma, and she is lying there in the hospital bed with all sorts of tubes and monitors. Then I look at her mom, who is sitting in the corner, covering her face with her hands, crying. She looks like nothing else other than destroyed. I set the lilies on a table in the room near the window before sitting next to Mrs. Ross. I wait for a moment before wrapping my arms around her. She takes a deep breath and makes a couple of loud sobs as she tries to speak.

"She's...Emma's..." She bends over even further toward her lap, still covering her face, before finishing her sentence. "My baby's in a coma." Upon finishing her words, she cries uncontrollably.

I gasp reactively and immediately want to ask a million questions, but she is in no condition to answer, let alone hear them. I grab the tissue box and bring it closer since now we both need it.

Shortly after calming back down to soft sobs and sniffles, a new doctor comes in to check on Emma. Mrs. Ross doesn't say anything as she watches the doctor review Emma's chart. Once the doctor steps out of the room, I follow her to ask my questions. "I feel terrible asking Mrs. Ross. Can you tell me what's going on?" I ask desperately.

Her eyes melt sympathetically as she answers, "There is no way to say this. She lost a lot of blood, and her brain was without oxygen for an extended amount of time. She is suffering from cerebral hypoxia."

"What does all that mean? Will she get better?" I ask, afraid of the answer.

"She is showing little brain activity. Depending on how much neuroplasticity she possesses, she may recover. It's possible there could be some permanent brain damage," the doctor says regrettably.

"When will we know? How long will she be in a coma for?" I ask with slight panic.

"It's hard to say in these cases. But typically, it can be a couple of months. In a lot of cases, the longer the coma lasts, the less chance of a happy outcome," she finishes before walking into another patient's room.

My mouth drops. I feel like I am screaming inside, but absolutely no one can help. There is no mercy to this feeling. The only thing to end it is for Emma to wake up. Now I understand why Mrs. Ross can hardly speak. She may never get the chance to speak with or hug her daughter again.

Needing a moment to think, I go down to the cafeteria to grab some lunch for Mrs. Ross and myself. When I arrive back to Emma's room with a food tray, I see Mrs. Ross staring out the window. It looks like she may have stopped crying, but her facial expression continues to look like mine, shocked.

"Here," I tell her. "You need to eat something."

She looks at me and smiles slightly before holding out her hand for her dish. "Thank you," she says barely clear enough to understand.

After she takes a few bites, I say, "I spoke to the doctor. I will be visiting her as often as I can. Please let me know of anything I can do or bring."

Mrs. Ross nods as we both finish our lunch. I stay at the hospital for as long as I am able before a nurse comes in and tells me that visiting hours are over for the day. "OK," I say, "I'll be back tomorrow. Goodbye, Emma. Goodbye, Mrs. Ross."

"Get home safe," Mrs. Ross replies.

The next day there is still no change with Emma when I arrive. I end up staying the entire day again, telling her stories of our childhood. There are quite a few that Mrs. Ross has enjoyed and a few she has scolded me for. Apparently, Emma didn't tell her mom a few of the rebellious ones. But her reactions to them make the stories even more fun to tell. If only Emma were awake to witness them.

Mrs. Ross remembers that Emma and I have planned a trip that we are supposed to be leaving for this coming weekend. "You have that trip coming up, right, Delilah?" she asks.

"Well, we did, but I won't be going now," I reply.

"Why not?" she asks. "It will do you good."

"Emma—" I start as she interrupts.

"You can't do any more for Emma being here than I can. What you can do is live the experience and bring back memories and pictures to share with her when she wakes up."

I think for a moment before responding, "You're right, Mrs. Ross. I need to go…for Emma. I'll be gone a few days, but I'll come visit next week."

"Go enjoy yourself and have fun. We'll be here when you get back," she says.

I wait again for visiting hours to end before leaving for home. Once I get through the door of my apartment, I pack for the trip, which is now only a couple of days out. After that I pour myself some wine and attempt to mentally prepare myself for going solo. I'm trying to be just as excited about going by myself as I would be with Emma, but I know that's an impossible goal.

Friday morning comes before I know it. I load up the car with my bags, making sure to pack an extra case of water. Emma never leaves the house without an extra case of water in the trunk. She has, through the years, drilled in my head that a car breaking down somewhere in Arizona without water is the last thing a person should want. Of course, she is absolutely correct. I used to never take more than a couple of bottles, but I took on Emma's routine a couple of years back. Now every time I throw a case in the trunk, I think of her.

Before leaving, I run back to my room and grab Emma's bright pink tennis ball. Tossing it up in my hands several times while walking to the car, I get in and place it in an empty cup holder and smile. She might be a part of this trip after all. Before getting on the highway, I make sure to top my tank off with gas and fill the tires with air. I am ready.

A little over four hours later, I arrive at my destination. I slowly get out of the car, stretching my legs as I stand up. My butt has officially gone numb from the drive. I don't dare look at my reflection in the side of the car, in fear of it possibly looking like a pancake. Taking a moment to breathe in the cooler air, I then look over at the Grand Canyon, and it is everything I have ever dreamed of, so breathtakingly big and full of colors.

After gathering all my hiking gear, I march my way down the Havasu Falls Trail from the Hualapai Hilltop. This should lead me all the way down to the bottom of the canyon. There is so much change in elevation back and forth while treading the first two miles. It's challenging, to say the least. I'm so glad I spent months training for this; otherwise, I'd be in trouble. After the warm welcome, the trail seems to be mostly flat for the next six miles. I then pass by three waterfalls: Fifty Foot, Lower Navajo, and the one I am most excited about, Havasu Falls.

Entranced by this mighty waterfall, I stare off as Damon slyly creeps into my thoughts. The last time I saw water nearly this powerful was on the beach with him and Emma. It has been months since a thought of him has crossed my mind. Yet he suddenly takes it over for several minutes before I hear a fish splash, bringing me back to present.

I stare at the waterfall for another moment before stepping into the five-foot-deep pool. As I walk closer, I can feel the water get deeper until just the tips of my toes touching the bottom are keeping my head afloat. The water is unbelievably blue and easily seventy degrees Fahrenheit. All my worries flow away as I stand here, feeling the immense power this waterfall has to offer. I cannot believe something so beautiful like this is only a few hours away from where I live. I could only imagine Emma's reaction to all this. She would be absolutely blown away. Good thing my camera has barely left my hand since getting out of my car. I will make Emma feel like she is really here by the time I'm done creating this album.

I am exhausted, and the campground is still a ways to go. So I pack up my things and journey on. Emma and I initially were going to sleep under the stars in our sleeping bags, but since I'm by myself, I luckily was able to book a room at the lodge. It was advised on the website to bring my own food to the campground, so I didn't pack the tastiest things but what would last and fill my belly: cans of chili, soup, crackers, and I threw in an avocado just to see how it works out. I open my sack, and the avocado is still perfectly formed, so I cut into it with my Swiss Army knife, peel it, and basically just eat it like an apple. Then I go for a can of soup before grabbing the bright pink tennis ball. I hold it as I go to lie on the bed. Then I toss it up toward the ceiling over and over again until I fall asleep.

The next day I hike back up north a bit to revisit Havasu Falls along with the other two. A passing hiker talks to me about Mooney Falls. It sounds so beautiful! I'll have to save that for when Emma is able to join in. Getting there sounds like too much of an adventure to do without her. While visiting the waterfalls, I take so many pictures that I can scroll and scroll through my camera roll before getting to any other content before this trip. These will definitely help Emma feel like she is here all along.

After my long weekend, I am ready to get back to my own bed. I pack up all my gear before checking out of the lodge. I respectfully look up at the path, remembering the difficult hike down here. My body is so worn out from playing in the waterfalls and hiking everywhere that it basically feels numb. In that case this hike back should be no problem, walking for the next week may be though, once the soreness kicks in.

Hours later, I finally make it to my car. I'm not ready to get on the road just yet. So I lean against the driver's side door for a little while to rest and take in the sights one last time before getting in. All I can think about is a big, fat, juicy burger and a bunch of fries. The perfect cherry on top would be an ice-cold Dos XX with extra lime. I can practically taste it. Motivated enough to get in the car, I'm on a mission to serve my taste buds after living off canned food in the last few days.

Shortly before reaching the highway to head home, I spot a Five Guys burger joint. Everything I need in life is right there through the doors. I quickly pull into a parking spot and rush inside to place my order. Once I receive my tray, I walk to a table, trying not to devour my meal on the way. I sit in my chair and scarf everything down in ten minutes before getting back on the road. The first thing I'm going to do when I get home is sleep for probably two days straight.

The drive back seems to take a lot longer than it did coming here, which is almost odd because there are zero cars on the road. I have the lanes completely to myself as I coast along. The views and turns through the mountains also make it interesting, so I really can't complain much.

As I pull under my covered parking at the apartment complex, I don't even feel like I'm home. I still feel like I'm at Havasu Falls, swimming in the pools. Once I unlock the door to my apartment, I drop all my luggage at the entrance and walk straight to the bathroom for a hot shower. When I dry off, I look at my bed. Those messy piles of sheets have never looked more comfortable. I crawl with my aching body under whatever covers I can grab with one hand before pulling them over and passing out two seconds later.

TEN

A week has gone by, and I am feeling refreshed and caught up with life. The only thing I have yet to do since I've been back from my trip is visit Emma. So I'm heading to a locally owned coffee shop near the hospital to grab a latte before spending the day with her.

When I enter the parking lot, I find a shady spot to park and get out of the car. The aroma of roasted coffee beans fills the air, and before taking another step, I breathe in deeply a few times. I can already feel the hot coffee migrating down my throat and webbing throughout my chest. I open the front door and walk straight to the cashier inside.

"Good morning!" the cashier greets. "What can I get started for you?"

I reply, "A large, hot caramel latte, please."

"Make that two," a strong voice adds. I turn around and see Officer Jones, Blake rather, towering above me, smiling. He takes out his card before I can say anything and pays for both orders.

"You must be following me," he suggests.

Caught off guard, I smile and say, "I could say the same thing to you."

He gives a quick laugh before asking, "What brings you over this way?"

"Oh," I say while taking a quick glance to the floor, "I am visiting Emma. She's still in the hospital."

He looks at me sympathetically before pulling out a chair at a nearby table and asking me to have a seat. I originally planned on grabbing my coffee and leaving, but it'd be nice to have someone to talk to. So I take a seat before he goes to grab both of our lattes. As we drink our coffee, we get lost in conversation. Two hours pass before I look at my phone and freak out at the time. Standing up, I say, "I have to get going. I can't believe I lost track of time. Thank you for the coffee."

"It was my pleasure. Here, I'll walk you out," he insists as he stands up, pushing himself up from the chair.

"OK," I reply and smile as we exit out the door.

Once we are at my car, I open my door and bend my knee to get in before he asks, "I know this may not be the best time, but are you doing anything this weekend?"

"Uh...I actually haven't made any plans yet," I say.

"I'll call you later this evening," he says.

"I look forward to it," I hesitantly respond with a frozen smile.

I sit in my seat before he closes my door behind me and walks off to his car. I watch him through my rearview mirror until he gets in. Then I turn on my engine, but before shifting gears, I find myself melting back in my seat. Just as I take a moment to feel excited about Blake, Damon enters my mind and hits me like a wall, blocking any thoughts of Blake. I haven't heard from him in months; how does he still have this much power over me? I shake the thoughts out of my head before shouting out loud, "No!" even though I am the only one who can hear it. Then I put my car in reverse and back out of my spot.

The hospital is only five minutes away; during the entire drive, I am battling my thoughts between Damon and Blake. Damon is everything I want, but in reality, he didn't want me bad enough to stay, not if he could just leave. What I feel for him he obviously couldn't reciprocate. I don't know him too well yet, but from what I've seen, Blake is strong, brave, respectful, handsome, and the list goes on. What's best about him? He is here.

I park in the visitor section at the hospital and walk through the entry doors and up the stairs to Emma's room with some fresh lilies in one hand and a photo book of my Havasu Falls trip in the other. I plan to keep it here for her to look at when she opens her eyes. For now I'll explain each and every photo and tell her lots of stories. If I explain it well enough, maybe she can visit while she's dreaming.

Mrs. Ross is the first thing I see upon entering Emma's room. She is holding Emma's hand, talking to her. Her voice is so low that all I can really make out are mumbles. It almost sounds like she is praying. I walk in, making sure not to disturb her, and take a seat by the window. When Mrs. Ross finishes talking, she looks up to me with tears in her eyes, forcing a small smile. I place the flowers and photo album on the seat next to me before standing up to give Mrs. Ross the most comforting hug I am capable of. With us being roughly the same height, she is easily able to nestle her face into my shoulder and I into hers. When I feel her tears drop onto my shirt, I cannot stop myself from also crying. After some slow breaths, she lifts her head and steps back. I grab some tissues for the both of us off the table.

While dumping the old flowers and filling the vase with fresh water, I ask Mrs. Ross, "Have there been any changes?"

"None," she says as she sniffles while folding the tissue to find another dry spot to wipe under her eyes.

There's nothing else I can think to say. No words seem right. I place the new flowers in the vase and carry them back to the window. Then I grab the photo book and sit next to Emma. I was going to wait until a little later to tell her about the trip, but Mrs. Ross can use a distraction. So can I to be honest. As I point to the pictures of the waterfalls, Mrs. Ross unknowingly changes her gloomy expression into a somewhat eager and hopeful one. She doesn't ask any questions, only looks to me with a hint of keen excitement, waiting for me to describe the next picture.

Once I finish, Mrs. Ross holds out her hand for the book, so I hand it over. She flips through all the pictures and sighs. "She would have loved to be there."

"She'll go, Mrs. Ross. I promised her. I'll make sure of it," I tell her with certainty before continuing, "It's Emma. She won't go before she's ready. You know she'll put up a fight like we've never seen."

Mrs. Ross can't do anything but cry. She knows I'm right. I reach out for more tissues and sit with them both a while longer. Then I lean in to give Mrs. Ross one last long hug before getting ready for home but not without the promise that I will be back in a few days.

"I know you will, but please call me if there are any changes. I will race over," I tell her before leaving Emma's room.

"You will know seconds after I do," she assures with a hopeful smile.

The moment I get into the door of my apartment, my phone rings. It's Blake! I forgot he said earlier that he was going to call me. I toss my purse and keys on the kitchen counter with so much force that they end up sliding off the other end. But there's no time to care about that right now. My only worry is answering this call before it goes to voice mail.

"Hello." I answer.

"Hey, Delilah, did I catch you at a good time?" Blake asks.

"You did actually. I was just walking in the door," I respond.

"Oh good," he says before continuing, "If you're still free for Saturday night, then I'd like to take you to dinner."

"Well, gosh, I guess that depends on where you have in mind," I reply playfully.

He gives a nervous laugh before saying, "Hard to impress, huh? I guess my cooking is out. I'm thinking a Brazilian steak house?"

I can't help but laugh. "Oooh! Hard to go wrong with that choice," I say.

"I'll take that as a yes?" he asks with hope.

"Absolutely," I say. "Pick me up at seven o'clock Saturday."

"I will be there," he says before ending the call.

After hanging up the phone, I can see Damon in the distance, racing toward my thoughts. I blink a few times and snap myself out of it. "Get lost, Damon," I say to myself as I imagine locking him out and throwing away the key.

Saturday is here. For whatever reason I am up way earlier than usual. That's OK, though, because quiet time on the patio with my coffee is something I look forward to. Normally, sleeping in is the only thing I want. But if I do happen to wake up this early, then making it outside to hear the birds' morning songs before hearing people steer their cars through the complex is all that comes to mind. I find it quite meditative.

The last drop of coffee spills from my mug into my mouth, and I'm finally ready to go back inside. Suddenly, I remember what today is and that Blake will be here later to pick me up. I must get ready! Of course, the day is still pretty young, so I'll take my time and make a day of it. I'm going to have some breakfast and then get a fresh mani-pedi for tonight.

As I take my first bite of cereal, I pick up my phone to call Emma. I scroll through my contact list and look for her name when it hits me that she's unable to pick up my call. My excitement drops a few notches. Entering a slump, I brush it off and drive to a nail salon by myself. This time I choose one that is close to my apartment. I love the one Emma and I always go to, but that has always been our spot to go together. It wouldn't feel right going there without her.

Walking into the nail salon, the staff all look up and talk to one another. By their mannerisms I can tell they know I'm not a regular. A lady pauses from giving someone a manicure and runs up to greet me. "Hello, what can I get you today?" she asks.

"I would like a mani-pedi if someone has time," I say.

The lady responds, "Oh yes, come take a seat in chair two," as she points to the pedicure chairs. "Someone will be over to help you in a minute."

I kick off my sandals and take a seat, dipping my feet in the warm spa. I get the massage chair going just the way I like, strong kneading, as I wait for my turn. With Emma not here, I should have brought a book or something. Not that I'd be able to flip through the pages, since I have another nail technician working on my hands.

I start thinking of all the events in the last few months involving Nick, Damon, and Emma. Is Blake going to be another sad ending? Is dating him worth the potential pain? What if it turns into something more beautiful than I could ever imagine? There's only one way to answer any of those. If Emma were here, she'd tell me to take a chance. She would say to "envision what I want, not what I fear." She has actually said that line to me so many times that it will be implanted in me probably for as long as I live.

"What color would you like?" a lady asks as I look down to see that I am already halfway through with my pedicure.

"Light pink," I say. "Add a black flower too, please." I think I'll mix it up a bit this time.

Getting my nails done without Emma is definitely not first choice, but it is still enjoyable. I can handle this for now; besides, this nail salon isn't too bad. Now I need to get back home and decide on what to wear for tonight.

After trying on roughly eight dresses, I find the one I think is best. This one is not too curve hugging because that is the last thing I want to wear when dining at a Brazilian steak house. If this wasn't a date, then I'd have on some stretchy pants to match the amount of food they serve. I pull the dress off the hanger and take a good look at it. It is flowy, mid-length, and dark pink in color. It has a scoop neck with a golden halter chain slipping through the front and around my neck. I'm going to wear my nude-colored stiletto heels and curl my hair. After all this he may not even recognize me seeing as all our meetings so far have consisted of me being a wreck either from being a damsel in distress or from simply rolling out of bed, deciding to stay in my sweats for the day while running errands.

I finish getting ready at about fifteen minutes to seven o'clock, just enough time for a glass of wine. Shortly after placing my empty glass on the counter, Blake knocks on the door. When I open it to see him in an outfit other than his police uniform, I am stunned. I didn't think he could be any more handsome. He must be having similar thoughts because, for once, I am not the only one having trouble finding words.

Blake clears his throat before holding his arm out for mine. "I am here to escort you to dinner, you gorgeous thing, you."

"You're such a dork," I say as I laugh and wrap my arm around his. He's funny. I like funny. Better yet, he opens the car door for me and closes it after I'm in.

It's about a ten-minute drive to the restaurant, and Blake is keeping conversation going so easily. He is a complete natural at making me feel open and comfortable around him. Once we are seated at our table, we get lost talking about another topic and then another before the server comes to take our drink order. The food comes, and we both are mostly quiet while we focus on the meal. I notice both of us taking a breath every now and then between bites to look at each other and smile. By the time we finish eating, I feel like I can barely stand up.

"I may have to waddle out of here," I tell him.

He laughs. "I will be waddling right behind you," he says as he signs the check. Then he stands up to pull out my chair for me to get up.

We arrive back at my apartment, but neither of us is ready to say goodbye. "Want to go for a walk?" I ask.

"That sounds perfect," he responds. "I can maybe walk off some of this meal."

We round the park on the other side of the complex, and thirty minutes later, we are back at my apartment. "Thank you for taking me out tonight," I tell him.

He smiles before asking, "Do you have plans next Saturday?"

"I don't," I reply.

"I'll plan on taking care of that then," he says. Then he leans into me and gives me a kiss on the cheek before giving me a strong good-night hug.

Once I lock my front door, I start thinking of that little cheek peck. Oh, how I wish his lips landed on mine. I know he chose not to out of respect, but he also totally did that on purpose with the intention of leaving me wanting more. It worked. I can't wait to tell Emma all about Blake when I see her in the morning.

The very first thing I do when I enter Emma's room is ask her mom for any updates while I place fresh flowers in the vase. She gives me the same answer every time. I am noticing this to be the usual pattern. Part of me thinks I should probably stop asking because I know it brings her pain having to say no. I just want to make sure that I don't miss any measurement of progress.

Blake is the first topic I bring up to Emma once I sit down beside her. He also happens to be the only topic. I guess I can say I'm excited about him. After about two more hours of visiting, I give Mrs. Ross a big hug before leaving.

"I'll be back again next Sunday," I tell them both.

"We will be here," Mrs. Ross replies.

ELEVEN

Three more months seem to practically fly by. I have been seeing Blake every Saturday and usually once during the week as well. He has been keeping pace with how fast I want our relationship to go. He will stay the night at my place and I at his, but we have yet to round third base. Holding out this long is so painful, especially since the last man I was with was Damon. But I am glad we are taking the time to really feel each other out before taking it to the next level. We haven't labeled ourselves as anything official, but we already kind of know how we feel. I am not interested in pursuing anyone else at this time, and I am sure he isn't either. All his attention is on me, and I couldn't be happier.

Visits with Emma have become naturally consistent on Sundays. I have created a pattern of showing up with fresh lilies as soon as I'm allowed to visit, dumping the old ones out, and filling the vase with clean water. I'll stay for two or three hours telling her about my time with Blake. I always make sure to share memories of our childhood too. Sometimes I will bring a book to read to her. She still shows absolutely no progress, but I know she is in there somewhere, trying to find her way out. Maybe if I spark some sort of memory, it may be enough stimulation to wake her up. That's my hope anyway.

Saturday arrives, and I wake up smiling, knowing that I'm going to see him a little later today. Blake bought us tickets for a Miranda Lambert concert downtown, and I couldn't be more ecstatic. I'm filling the time beforehand by blasting every song I can find of hers on my Bluetooth speaker while I dance and sing around the apartment. I grab a broom and then a mop and clean the entire place in no time. I light some candles for a finishing touch. Then I shower before doing some yoga in the living room. I don't know how or when doing these things became a date ritual, but this combination of acts always puts me in the sexiest, most feel-good mood. As much as I love a good dress for date nights, tonight I am pulling out my tight jeans with rhinestones, complemented by my Dan Post boots and cowgirl hat. I even throw on a crop top similar to the one Emma wore on our beach vacation. If she could see me right now, she'd be proud.

Blake arrives to pick me up, and I see that he and I are on the same page. Here he is wearing authentic cowboy boots and matching hat. Again, I can't do anything but stare at how handsome he is. He can literally pull off any look.

He looks me up and down before saying, "You are such a looker," as he gives me a kiss.

Blushing, I reply, "Oh stop. I just threw on whatever was clean," even though I dug down to the bottom of my drawers for this specific crop top.

He laughs as he puts his arm around me while we walk to the passenger side of his car. He opens the door for me. "Watch your hat," he jokes as I get in.

"Watch yours," I say as I try to flip it off his head. But he catches my hand and pulls me in for a kiss.

"Now get in," he demands with a smile.

"Yes, Officer," I reply.

Blake laughs as he closes my door and walks around to his side. The drive to downtown is easily thirty minutes, and that's without a concert going on, backing up traffic. But as excited as we both are to get there, I also wish this car ride would last longer. I have the best time simply sitting here with him. We don't even have to say anything, and I enjoy it just as much.

The concert, her voice, and the drinks are out of this world but pricey. I don't expect anything less at a concert, which is why I snuck in some little liquor shot bottles in my boots. I'm sure it's not a big deal as I have done this probably 102 times. But if it happens to be one, then Blake can handcuff me if he wants. I won't be mad. Carefully, I bend over to take one out of the inside of my left boot and twist off the cap. He looks at me from the corner of his eye before quickly turning his head, fully facing me, looking at my hands. He waits for a second before saying anything.

"Hey," he says, "are you going to share or what?"

"Well, I guess I have to now since I got caught and all." I laugh as I take another out of my right boot and hand it over.

Walking out to his car after the concert, I am feeling kind of buzzy. He still looks as sober as a judge. Good thing he's driving. We make it back to my apartment, and I invite him to stay the night as we've basically made a habit of doing that on Saturdays anyway. He walks to my room to get ready for bed as I go to the kitchen to grab us both some water.

When I enter through the doorway, I see him lying on top of the bed in nothing but his briefs. I swear he could easily be a Calvin Klein model. This sight is something I look forward to every Saturday. It's part of what helps me make it through the week. I hand him his water before placing mine on the nightstand. Then I walk to the bathroom to brush my teeth. I come back out, and he is watching me make my way around the room, hang up my sweater, and grab pajamas out of the dresser drawer. His eyes don't veer away as I push my jeans down my legs to the floor and wiggle out of them. After throwing them in the laundry basket, I take a quick look at him and catch him still staring at me. Blushing, I turn away from him to take off my shirt and bra.

I hear the bedspring squeak as he gets up to walk over to me. He places his rough yet warm hands on my shoulders, slowly turning me around. His hands remain in place as he looks me over before kissing me. "Don't hide," he says before continuing to kiss me more. He is gently pushing me, making me stumble a couple of feet backward, and eventually, the backs of my legs are against the bed frame.

His hands travel down my arms before migrating to my waist. Still kissing me, he softly lays me down on the bed. He crawls in bed beside me, laying one arm under my head and the other across my stomach. His fingertips glide across the inside of my pelvis as they make their way down to fondle me. He waits for me to squirm before sliding them fully inside. My eyes close, and I am arching my back from the pleasure while gripping the sheets with both hands. I feel his warm mouth find my nipple, and he begins sucking while flicking the tip with his tongue.

I'm getting close to climax, and he throws me on top of him, not stopping his fingers from arousing me as he replaces them with his erection. I rock back and forth, feeling every inch of him moving in and out of me. His moans grow louder as I begin to climax. He just finished but is still thrusting, making sure I get mine too, which I do in a matter of seconds. It is the longest orgasm I have had in a long time. It completely wipes me out, making me fall to the bed beside him. He pulls me in and kisses my lips before kissing my forehead. As tired as we both are, neither of us can fall asleep right away after. We are both laying here, staring up at the ceiling. I am replaying everything tonight, especially what we just did two minutes ago. That is definitely the highlight of my evening, and I'm very sure it is his too.

In the morning we are woken up by a call from Mrs. Ross. "Sorry for calling so early," she stammers. "I just received some news from the doctor, and I wanted to let you know before you head down here today."

I stop breathing for a moment before asking, "What happened? Is something wrong?"

Mrs. Ross stutters as she forces the words out, "Emma has had some changes in brain activity."

"Well, that's great, isn't it?" I utter. "I will be there in twenty minutes tops."

"No, Delilah," she says regrettably, "her brain is showing a decrease in the little activity it already had."

"Mrs. Ross?" I say, urging her to continue.

"It is only a matter of time, Delilah. My baby is leaving me," Mrs. Ross says as she begins crying hysterically on the other end.

Immediately feeling overwhelmed, not one thought enters my mind. The only thing I am capable of doing is giving the reactive response of "I'm coming" before hanging up. I uncontrollably burst into tears myself. Blake was lying close enough to hear the entire conversation. He doesn't say anything but instead pulls me in and holds on to me for as long as it takes my tears to stop.

"Would you like a ride to the hospital?" he asks with complete empathy.

Wiping my tears, I respond, "Thank you, but I will be OK. I just need to shower and collect my thoughts. I'll walk you out when you're ready."

He smiles slightly before putting his clothes on and walking to the front door, holding me close. As he goes to unlock the dead bolt, he says, "There is nothing I can say to make any of this better, but I'm here if you need anything."

"Thank you," I tell him quietly as I look at the floor.

He places his hand under my chin and softly lifts it to look into my eyes. "I will check on you later," he assures. I nod and form a faint smile before he turns around and walks to his car.

After closing the front door, I find myself staring at absolutely nothing as I cannot believe any word Mrs. Ross just said. There is no way it's true. Life without Emma? I've never pictured it. She has been with me every step of the way in life so far. Mrs. Ross is mistaken. I'm going to throw myself together, grab a bundle of lilies, and head down there to get a complete understanding of what is going on. There is no time for breakfast, so I grab a protein bar and apple to eat along the way.

I arrive at the hospital just as visiting hours start and rush to Emma's room faster than I ever have. Mrs. Ross is already working on her third box of tissues this morning. Before anything else, I replenish the vase with the fully bloomed white lilies I have bought along the way. Just as I am about to say something, a doctor enters the room whom I don't recognize. I could have sworn I have met them all by now. He glances at the chart and monitors. I lose my ability to breathe as I watch him look over the numbers. Why isn't he saying anything? Give me something at least!

"Doctor," I finally ask impatiently, "can you tell me what's going on?"

The doctor looks at Mrs. Ross for approval. After Mrs. Ross tells the doctor I am family, he becomes an open book. "There is no longer any hope for Emma," he says. "Her brain is going the opposite direction of what we have been hoping for. Technically, she's dying."

"What do you mean dying? Look at her. She's young and healthy. She even looks strong," I say in panic.

The doctor's face shows even more sympathy as he says, "There is more damage than her brain is able to repair."

"What does that mean?" I ask. "What happens now?"

The doctor takes one more breath before saying, "It's only a matter of time before her brain shows no activity, a lot of times within twenty-four hours. She will be declared brain-dead. Without artificial life support, her body has zero chance of survival."

I don't say anything. I can't. My mouth drops open as the doctor leaves the room. My eyes flood with so much water as I look at Mrs. Ross that all I can see is a blurry blob of colors. The tears can't even be blinked out this time. I walk over to Emma's bed and fall across her lap, weak. My entire world is falling apart as I bury my face in her blanket and cry, gripping her sheets with my hands. "It's not too late, Emma. Please come back to us. I'm right here. I'm not going anywhere, and you better not either," I beg her desperately. Then I feel a hand glide up and down my back.

Mrs. Ross stood up from her seat to walk over and comfort me. The only thing either of us can do right now is comfort each other as we watch the rest of Emma slip away completely out of our control.

There is no way I can leave the hospital, let alone her room. Any moment may be her last, and I'm not letting her go through it without me here next to her. Besides, Mrs. Ross needs me, and I need her.

Four hours later Emma is showing barely any brain activity. Blake has texted me to make sure I am OK, but I haven't responded yet. I am not going to miss any of these seconds I have left with Emma.

I briefly look down at my hands while praying to the universe to give us the strength to get through this. The room is very quiet besides the sounds of our sobs along with the monitors. We both can't stop staring at Emma. She is so young and beautiful. Her long, light brown, curly hair is in a single braid, lying along her neck and draping over her shoulder. I have not seen her hazel eyes open at all in weeks. As I continue gazing over her fair, porcelain skin, I recognize a familiar scar engraved on her forearm from when she fell from a tree when we were little. I have a matching one from attempting to catch her, also falling as a result. I ended up nicking the same branch she did.

Thinking of that memory and how fun a day it was, I smile as I get lost in it.

Suddenly, I hear an alarm from the monitors. Mrs. Ross's cries grow louder as I look at the screen to see Emma's heart rate flatlining. A nurse runs in, followed shortly by the doctor, to check all the connections and vitals.

"Time of death," the doctor says as he looks at the clock, "2:42 p.m."

I fall to my knees, screaming, "No, Emma! Please no!"

My face falls in my hands as I cry and ask whoever is up there listening, "Why Emma? Why her? You made a mistake. Please take me, please."

Mrs. Ross can't do anything but fall back in the chair, trying to hide from the world. The doctor walks out as the nurse stays behind to comfort Mrs. Ross with hugs and endless amounts of tissues.

Eventually, the nurse also leaves. Mrs. Ross and I are barely able to compose ourselves as we sit here next to Emma almost in silence but for sure in disbelief. Every memory, even the ones when we were in diapers, comes pouring in my mind. A flashback of our entire lives plays like a movie in my head that lasts for two straight hours. It would have lasted longer, but it's interrupted when a nurse comes in with final paperwork.

I stay with Mrs. Ross as she wraps up the final stack of papers regarding plans for Emma's body. Then we both become each other's anchor of support as we force ourselves out of Emma's room. We remain holding each other up as we make it down what seem like never-ending hallways while we make our way toward the exit. We stagger out the doors into the parking lot, and Mrs. Ross has a friend waiting outside for her with a car since she is in no shape to drive. I give her a hug goodbye as she offers to take me home. I really need to be alone to process this, so I decline before letting her know that I will talk to her soon. Then I walk to my car on the other end of the parking lot.

I get in and buckle my seat belt. Before turning my key in the ignition, I think of Emma. Staring out of the parking lot at the main road and all the cars passing by, I continue to be engulfed in disbelief. I saw her take her last breath, but I still don't believe she is gone. I find myself sitting here for another hour or so, crying uncontrollably one moment and being fine in another. After a long while, I am able to compose myself enough to drive home. Almost back at my complex, Blake tries to call me, but I have no strength to speak, so I screen his call.

I'm a complete wreck for the rest of the evening. I place my phone on the kitchen counter before going to bed and forget about it. Blake tries calling me once more, following it with a text saying he is worried, but I don't hear it. All through the night, I have a terrible time sleeping. If I'm not having nightmares involving Emma, then I am waking up in panic from the memory of losing her. Eventually, I cry myself back to sleep, and the pattern continues.

It is late into the morning before I wake and grab my phone off the kitchen counter. Taking it back in bed with me, I notice all of Blake's contact attempts. Only a moment later, there's a knock on my door, so I force myself out of bed to see who it is. It's Blake. I'm so depressed that I don't care at all how I look right now. So I answer the door to let him in. He looks at me for a moment before stepping inside and taking me in his arms.

"Go lie down," he says. "I'm going to make you something to eat."

I whimper as I walk to the couch instead of my room. Thank goodness he is here. I don't know how he knew I needed him, but I definitely do. Being in the same room as him may help comfort me and ease my mind. Watching him move about the kitchen, opening drawers and cupboards, I notice how well he knows his way around. He's only had to search through my cupboards a handful of times for something like a water glass or fork. "You really know your way around the kitchen," I say.

"Maybe a little," he modestly replies with a smile.

He gets a small smile out of me before I say, "And there you were, making me believe you were a bad cook all this time."

"Don't be so sure yet. These pancakes and bacon may smell good, but it all depends on the taste test," he says.

"I'm not going to go easy on you then," I tell him.

"Good, I wouldn't want you to," he says while looking at me smiling.

He brings a plate over to me as I remain sitting on the couch. I instantly scarf it down without coming up for air. "This is amazing." I tell him.

He laughs and replies, "You probably just haven't eaten since yesterday morning before going to the hospital."

Taking a moment to think, I respond, "Oh my gosh, you're right. So me basically being at the point of almost willing to eat anything doesn't really say much about your cooking, huh?"

He gives a small laugh before answering, "Not really, but you're still eating it, so I'll take it."

After spending most of the morning together, Blake has to leave for work. He gives me a kiss, telling me he will call once his shift ends. "Make sure you answer this time," he asserts in a lighthearted way.

I present him with a small laugh and tell him, "I will. I promise."

After giving him a kiss goodbye, I walk slowly back inside to clean up the dishes in the sink that I had told him to leave. Any distraction is welcome right now as long as it helps keep me from thinking of Emma.

TWELVE

Exactly one week later, I get a call from Mrs. Ross. We've been talking just about every day, but this is the call I have been both dreading and waiting for, funeral arrangements for Emma. There won't be a formal funeral because Mrs. Ross had her cremated in hopes of spreading her ashes in all the places she has loved. Until those places can be decided, there will be a nontraditional celebration of life ceremony. Emma wouldn't have wanted everyone to be dressed in black, moping around. She was such an uplifting and joyous person that she'd simply want us to throw a party. So that is exactly what we plan on doing. I want to set up a slideshow that can display pictures and clips of Emma through the years as we all share memories of her with one another. Even though she won't physically be there, she will still fill the room with love and cheer.

We send invites out to all her family and friends. The celebration of life party will be held on a Saturday two weeks from today. Mrs. Ross asks me if I want to send notice to Damon. I haven't thought of him in forever. I tell her it would be better for her to do since he and I have lost communication in the past months. She doesn't need to be made aware of all the details, especially right now. I will surely invite Blake though. After all, I'm probably going to need his strong arms to hold me up at some point during the event.

There is a lot to get done in a matter of two weeks, so I stick by Mrs. Ross and help set up in any way I can. I'm pretty much on call. Among other tasks, she puts me in charge of the playlist. The first songs I can think of adding are the ones Emma would traditionally sing at karaoke. She sang a lot of songs by various female country artists, so I look through several albums, adding all the ones I've heard her either sing or play on repeat. Blake is delighted to receive an invitation, not that I'll give him a choice in going or not. He plans on picking me up on the day of the event for a ride over. It works out perfectly because that means he can help me haul stuff over. He'll be thrilled!

It's the day of the ceremony, and I wake up knowing that after today, I will be one step closer to having closure with Emma's passing. I throw on bright colors to wear in an attempt to make it a happy occasion, even though I know everyone at the ceremony will be mostly swamped with sorrow. When Blake arrives to my apartment, he comes to my door to help me bring final decorations along with a few other items out to the car.

We arrive about five minutes late to the venue. Blake follows me in with the supplies and sets them on a table for Mrs. Ross. I can't believe the number of guests who are here so far. The place is already filled wall to wall with people, so much so that many have spilled their way out to the patio for air. Of course, I know she is always loved; I really have no idea how many people she actually touched with her life before walking into this room. With all these people possessing similar love for her as I have, it's easy to feel connected to her just by being around them all. I walk through the crowd, hearing different stories being told. It is the most comforting feeling.

After roughly an hour of everyone settling in and getting to know one another, I take the stage in front of the projector that is displaying the images of Emma. I grab hold of the microphone and first thank everyone for being here. Then I continue to share how I met Emma and everything she means to me. As I peer through the crowd, seeing familiar faces, my eyes stop moving when they land on Damon. He is standing so still compared with everyone else, giving me his undivided attention while I'm almost at the end of my speech. I am left stunned. Barely able to make the rest of my words out, I bring my speech to a close before handing off the microphone to the next person.

My breathing pattern changes, and my heart sinks. He's here. While making my way toward the stage's exit, all the memories of Damon that I thought had been forgotten suddenly come rushing back. I wish it was only the memories, but that passion and fire accompanies them and burns even stronger than before.

Stepping down from the stage with my eyes still locked with Damon's, the entire venue disappears, taking the crowd with it. I see a straight path leading to him. My feet take one step after the other a few times before I even realize I am walking toward him. I still have his full attention. Roughly five feet away, my lips part to say something, but Blake is suddenly at my side, which brings me to an abrupt stop. I honestly forgot he was here for a moment because he, too, disappeared along with the crowd. Damon's facial expression goes from hopeful excitement to curious uncertainty. Is he threatened? He is the one who didn't take a chance with me when he had it, so that's his problem.

My sudden hesitancy to continue walking doesn't deter Damon from walking the rest of the way to meet me. "Hello," he says.

I am unsure how to respond. Not wanting to make anything awkward, I play the part and say, "Oh hi, Damon, this is Blake." I turn to Blake. "And this is Damon, Emma's cousin." I smile and leave it at that. If nothing else, he connects me to Emma, and because of that, I need him in my life, even as nothing more than a friend.

Blake responds, "Oh yes, I remember you from that night outside the karaoke lounge dealing with Delilah's ex-boyfriend." He must have forgotten that Damon had his arm around me that night when he arrived at the scene. He either forgot or thought nothing of it.

"Oh, that's why you look familiar. Thank you for being there that night," Damon replies.

Blake looks at me before wrapping one arm around my waist and responds, "It was fate," then looks back at Damon and continues, "Good to see you again," before asking me if I'd like a drink from the refreshment table.

"I would love one," I tell him. Damon keeps his eyes on him as he walks off to make his way through the maze of people and head toward the other side of the venue.

Damon and I are awkwardly quiet for a moment before I decide to break the silence. "So they gave you military leave for the funeral, huh?"

"They did," he says. "Normally, that's reserved for immediate family, but I told them she was basically my sister. It helps that I'm well liked over there because they made an exception."

"Well, that works out nice," I say casually. "How long are you here for this time?"

He looks down at his boots. "I leave to go back tomorrow," he answers. Again, I am quiet and pretend to be unfazed. Of course, he has to leave again so soon. He's good at leaving.

Damon looks at me for a moment, deciding what to say. He finally asks the question that I know has been on his mind. "How long have you two been seeing each other?"

"Roughly four or five months now," I respond, smiling slightly.

"Does he make you happy?" he asks.

"Yes," I answer firmly as Blake walks back to us with our drinks. Damon tries to catch my eyes as I purposefully look away. I can make my face appear indifferent, but eyes are harder to mask. So I look away before he can get a read.

As soon as Blake stands back at my side, Damon looks at the two of us and says, "It was nice seeing you both again," before walking away to speak with other guests.

I cannot take my eyes off him until Blake says, "Mrs. Ross has the microphone," while pointing to the stage.

I look up as she shares memories of Emma all the way back from when she was a baby. She even tells stories involving me. How could I not be in them? Emma and I did everything together. She probably had more shared memories with me than without as I with her. By the time I see Mrs. Ross come down from the stage, I am wiping tears off my cheeks derived from her emotional account of her memories. I glance around the room for Damon, but I don't see him anywhere. He's extraordinarily good at not being seen when he doesn't wish to be. I'm sure he wouldn't leave so soon, but he keeps his distance if not.

Shortly before the celebration of life ceremony ends, I make my way to say goodbye to Mrs. Ross. "Wait, Delilah," she says. "I have something for you." She goes to her things on a table reserved for everyone's belongings and pulls out a small wooden box with a carved-out heart bearing Emma's name in the middle.

She holds it out to me and says, "You knew Emma probably better than anyone. Please put some of her ashes in a place she loved that will always bring her to mind when visiting."

Covering my mouth with my hand, I begin, "Mrs. Ross, I wouldn't know the first place."

"Take your time, Delilah. It will come to you. Wherever you choose will be perfect," she finishes.

I smile as I grip the box in my arms against my chest, trying not to cry. "Thank you, Mrs. Ross. This means so much to me."

"It would to her too," she responds with a smile.

I walk over to Blake, who is waiting by the exit to take me home. I don't even try looking for Damon again as I leave. Blake opens the passenger side door of his car, and I get in. Then I lay the box on my lap before he closes the door behind me and makes his way around to his side. I trace my fingers around the heart before sliding my hands over the top and down the sides as I whisper, "Emma." When he gets in, he sees teardrops landing on the box's surface. Before starting the car, he leans over without saying anything. He gives me a tight hug and kisses my cheek.

Once we arrive at my apartment, Blake walks me to the door. All I want is to be alone tonight, so I don't invite him in. He is so sweet and understanding. Before leaving, he gives me one more kiss, letting me know he will call me in the morning.

I walk into the common area, still holding the wooden box with both hands. There is not one place I can think of to spread Emma's ashes. I love every single place I have ever been to with her. How can I possibly choose? At least that decision doesn't need to be made tonight. For now I will place her on the wooden console above the television.

THIRTEEN

Fast-forward to around six months after Emma's death. Our annual beach vacation is coming up, and even though Emma will not be a part of it, it is something I don't want to miss. Blake has become a major constant in my life, so I invite him to come with me. That way I am not entirely alone. Plus, he and I are getting serious enough; it's about time we have a getaway.

I make sure to book the usual room, 103. It sells itself with its straight path to the water. After Blake and I put our things down, we rush out to the beach toward the ocean. We walk along the wet sand, collecting shells, while the water rushes under our feet, feeling the remnants of the waves come and go.

Our walk leads us to the pier on the other end of the beach. Blake grabs my hand and walks me up the sandy hill leading to the pier's entrance. As we walk along the pier toward the blue open view, the sun begins to set. We make it to the very end and stare off into the distance while standing next to each other quietly. As the sun goes down, a bunch of colors mesh in the sky, at times showing bright, vibrant orange streaks, which are probably my favorite part.

The sun is barely peeking over the water as it says its final farewell for the day. Blake turns to face me, holds both of my hands, and asks, "Will you be my girlfriend?"

I smile at how corny he is as I reply, "I would like nothing more," before leaning forward to kiss him.

After walking back to our room from the pier, we get ready to go out for a nice dinner with champagne to celebrate. I feel like I am having a honeymoon type of high for the rest of our trip. I can't believe we're actually an item. He is absolutely perfect. How did I get so lucky?

Two days later it is time to leave this beach utopia and make the drive home. We load up the car, throw in a case of water, and get on the road.

During the next six months, Blake and I continue to become more serious. We have been spending most nights together taking turns in staying between his place and mine. Last night was one of those nights where I wanted to be alone in my own bed. There is no reason to it; sometimes I enjoy my own space. I start making breakfast in the kitchen when Blake messages me. "My parents are coming in town this weekend. I would like for them to meet you. My place for dinner?" he says.

I take a moment to respond. This is a huge step, but I do see myself moving forward with him. So I guess this is inevitable. I respond, "I can't wait!"

When I arrive to Blake's house for dinner, his mom is already standing in the doorway, smiling in an attempt to hide that she is eyeing me down with intense judgment. I know this by the way she is tightly folding her arms together in front of her chest. Of course, I don't blame her.

Every mom probably feels threatened in some sort of way about the new woman in her baby's life.

"Hello, Mrs. Jones. I am Delilah," I say politely as I reach out my hand to her.

Instead of reaching her hand back, she unfolds her arms, throwing them both up in the air, coming straight in for a hug. "It is so wonderful to meet you, my dear!" she exclaims. She then walks me into the dining room to meet her husband, Mr. Jones. "Dear, this is the young lady Blake has been raving about all these months."

I turn to look at Blake and catch him blushing even harder than I am. I laugh as I say, "It is very nice to meet both of you, Mr. Jones."

"Who's hungry?" Blake interrupts.

I jump at the distraction. "Oh, I am!"

"Let's all get to the kitchen table and sit down," Mrs. Jones says before we all make our way to our seats.

Dinner is pleasant and comical as Blake's parents take turns sharing stories of him when he was younger. They are the same embarrassing stories that every parent tells about their child. Besides the associated embarrassment, these types of stories always make for a good time. I'm just glad my mom isn't here to partake also.

A while after dinner, Blake walks me out as his mom shouts, "Make sure you bring that one around more often, Blake! She's a keeper!"

He blushes as he turns back to see me also basking in the embarrassment. All I can do is giggle as I thank him for dinner and kiss him good night. "Thank you for inviting me," I tell him.

He laughs and says, "Thank you for coming and being a good sport. They are a lot sometimes."

I laugh as I reply, "They are absolutely wonderful."

During the entire drive home, I find myself smiling at how successful dinner was. Meeting the parents always makes me anxious, but it helps that they seem to approve of me dating their son. As fun of a time as that was, I am immensely glad it's over with.

A few days later, I receive an unexpected letter in the mail. There's a return address in the corner that I recognize as where Damon was stationed, Hickam Air Force Base in Oahu. I walk inside to the kitchen counter and open a drawer, looking for the letter opener. I stick the letter opener inside a small corner of the envelope and take a deep breath as I slide it from the top toward the bottom, opening it at the side. When I pull it out, I read:

Dear Delilah,

I have not been able to stop thinking of you since the first moment we said goodbye. I was hoping to apologize when I saw you at the ceremony. I don't want it left unsaid, so from the bottom of my heart, I want to apologize for the pain I have caused you. There is nothing I can say to make things right since I cannot take back my actions. I hope you can find in your heart to forgive me. I also wish to be able to keep writing to you, if you don't mind. I want for you and me to remain friends. After all, Emma's family is my family.

I miss you,
Damon

I drop my hand holding the letter into my lap. Should I write back to him? If I do, what should I say? Giving myself a long moment to think, I decide I must write him back. After all, he deserves some sort of answer. But what?

I take a few days to think of something worthy of a postage stamp before picking up a pen and paper and letting whatever thoughts come to mind be written.

> *Dear Damon,*
>
> *I forgive you. I also want to apologize for how I left things when I was angry. Since Emma's passing, you have become even more important for me to hold on to. You are someone I would never want to lose. You are my family as much as she was. I forgive you.*
>
> *Keep writing to me,*
> *Delilah*

The next day I walk with the letter to the outgoing mailbox at the front office of my apartment complex. I hold it tightly against my chest one last time before dropping it in the slot.

On the walk back, I receive a call from Blake. "Hey, Delilah, what are you up to?" he asks. I am honestly not sure how he would feel about my pen pal, so I won't bring it up for now. What Damon and I had in the past is over. I want to keep him around but for different reasons. He makes me feel close to Emma, and I will do anything to keep a connection to her.

I respond, "Just taking a morning walk around my complex," which isn't entirely a lie.

"I am going to come pick you up for a lake day in roughly two hours. Got my boat ready along with two paddleboards. Get your things together!" he says adamantly.

I shriek, "That sounds like so much fun! See you soon."

Now rushing back to my apartment, I scurry through my drawers and closet, piling up everything I will need on my bed before grabbing my light blue beach tote. After stuffing the pile inside it, I run to the bathroom to curl my hair. I'm not too sure why since the boat will mess it up anyway. But maybe I will be lucky enough to get a few good pictures in before that happens.

Paddleboards are my absolute favorite. All the water activities are fun, but this one in particular always makes my eyes light up. Once we get to Blake's favorite cove in the lake, we toss out the paddleboards into the water before getting onto them.

"This is the best spot in the entire lake," he praises.

"Why is that?" I ask curiously.

He stares at me for a moment before looking around. "For whatever reason, not a whole lot of people come in this section. It's pretty secluded, bringing me that peace I desire when out on the water."

I look at him as I chuckle. "I know what you mean," before continuing, "Emma and I enjoyed doing that with kayaks in the ocean. We'd go so far out from civilization." Being caught up in the memory, I can't help myself from gazing off.

He leads me to this little path of water flowing in between the mountain walls. It's almost untouched since boats and Jet Skis are unable to fit back here. I follow him through its shallow waters. Once we are far enough to where I can no longer see the way we came in, I lay tummy down on the paddleboard and gaze down to watch all the little fish swimming through the algae and the tall grass bending in the light current.

I sit up on my paddleboard to see Blake paddling his board toward me. He lines his up to mine and carefully lifts me onto his with him. He brushes my hair from my face before laying his lips on mine. Just as we are getting handsy, the paddleboard tips over, making us fall in the water. Thankfully, where we land isn't too deep, and the rocks are smooth, so we only end up getting drenched, which made this even more enjoyable. We both sit up out of the water, laughing as we get back onto both of our paddleboards. Then we paddle back to the boat for lunch.

For the entire time we eat, we are both giving each other the same look of wanting to continue what we were doing out on the paddleboards. As soon as we finish up our plates, he takes them both and throws them into the trash bag that he has tied to the inside of the boat. Then he comes back for me, lifting me and carrying me straight down to the cabin.

Not even fully down the steps, he puts me down and continues kissing me like he did before we went for an involuntary swim. He unties the back of my bikini top as I work on undoing the tie of his swimming trunks. Once we are both naked, he pushes me up against the cabin wall and cups my breasts in each hand, squeezing them while massaging my tongue with his. Without stopping, he lures me to the bed and throws me down, making sure my legs remain hanging off. I watch him get down to his knees in front of me and wrap my legs over the back of his shoulders as his tongue runs up my inner thigh. He spends his time tracing my hot spot, making me pulse from the craving. Once he feels he has tortured me enough, his tongue finally enters me, making me go wild. Just as I am reaching climax, he quickly jumps on top of me, shoving his full erection inside before pulling it back out over and over again. I can't stop myself from letting out a scream as I orgasm loud enough for passing boats to hear. Good thing we are the only ones in this part of the lake.

After a long and active day, we pull the boat to the docks before driving back to my place for dinner. We are so burned out that we call in for pizza instead of cooking and call it a night after taking down every last bite.

FOURTEEN

Two weeks later I receive another letter in the mail from Damon. It is basically describing his time in Oahu and telling me of new experiences. Part of me feels guilty for writing letters back to him because of what I have going on with Blake. On the other hand, even though he doesn't ask about Blake in the letters, he saw me with him at Emma's celebration, so he knows I'm with him. Damon may not be happy about it, but I know he'll still respect it. He really has no choice.

In the coming months, Damon and I remain pretty consistent in sending letters to each other roughly every two weeks. Sometimes he can't get one to me right away and will end up sending two at a time once he has access to a mailbox again. To be honest I have come to really look forward to his letters. Talking to someone who enjoyed Emma in the same ways as I did feels comforting. I can almost feel her in every word he writes.

I ended up telling Blake about the letters several weeks ago, and he actually took it better than I expected. I even showed him a couple of them since I save them all. He didn't seem threatened by it at all, which made me feel at ease writing to Damon as often as I want. He knows I also keep up with the rest of Emma's family, so it's not entirely out of the norm. Mrs. Ross and I still message each other just about every day as well.

Blake calls me up on a Sunday afternoon, wanting to take me on a shopping spree. He is so wonderful, always spoiling me out of the blue. The mall is closer to his place, so I meet him at his house before carpooling. As we take our time window-shopping, Blake looks down at every jewelry counter we pass. I notice his sight continuously falling to the section filled with engagement rings, but I remain oblivious. I don't want him to realize that I know exactly what he is doing.

"Oh look! There is Victoria's Secret. Come on!" I say as I pull him along.

When we get into the store, I walk him over to the lingerie section and look at him while I say, "Well?"

"Well what?" he asks.

"If you're the one who is paying, you should be the one who decides what I wear for you," I coyly answer.

He blushes with excitement and picks one of each item off the rack for me to try on. My eyes grow big at all his selections as he piles them in my arms and pushes me toward the fitting room.

"I'll be right outside the door," he says as he rushes me into the closest room. I come out modeling each piece one at a time with a little spin. I see his jaw drop further and further to the ground with every piece. This instantly became one of my favorite dates, pure entertainment for the both of us, and I get to go home with some sexy new attire.

All this shopping works up an appetite, so we leave the mall to go back to his place for a bite to eat while he carries the shopping bags. He offers to make tacos, something I have trouble refusing. But I know he probably just can't wait to get me home to model my new purchases some more.

I was right; as we walk through the door, he shuffles his hands through my bag, pulling out the red lace set at which his eyes really widened back at the store. "Put these on while I make dinner," he says, "with nothing over it."

Looking at him for a moment, I blush at the request. We have seen each other naked plenty of times, but I never pranced around the room in basically nothing for the entire evening in front of him. Although slightly nervous, I'm feeling quite exhilarated. It's hard to be bored around him, that's for sure.

I come out of his room wearing exactly what he has requested, and he stops cooking for a moment to come grab and kiss me. After giving me a taste of what's in store for later, he walks back to the kitchen, turning off the burners before fixing both of our plates. Before sitting down at the table, he looks me up and down, grinning like a kid in a candy store.

"I guess I better strip down to my undergarments as well," he says, laughing as he pulls his shirt off over his head. Then he opens the button to his pants before undoing the zipper, pulling them down to his ankles and kicking them off. I could easily watch all that at least five more times.

After dinner he gets up from his chair and walks over to me as I remain sitting. He leans down for a kiss as he places one hand softly around my neck. Still kissing him, I stand up, and he leads me to the couch. He lies down with me on top of him as he kisses me more, running his hands all over my body, slipping the bra straps off my shoulders.

My hands run down his sides toward his waist when his phone rings.

I cannot hear who is on the other end, but I hear him loud and clear when he says that he is on his way before hanging up. He looks at me and says regrettably, "Sorry, Delilah. I'm finishing up a case at work, and they need me to come in."

"Don't be sorry," I utter. "I've had you all day. I can share a little."

He gives me a kiss before getting ready for work. Once we are both dressed, we leave his place together, and he walks me to my car.

"We will pick this up tomorrow," he says while smiling.

"I can't wait," I say excitedly. And we did just that.

A few days later, there is a letter from Damon in the mail. I want more than anything to sit down and read it, but I am already running late for lunch with Blake. So I walk back from the mailbox to my apartment and place the letter in the drawer of my bedside table. I will pull it out later tonight when I can give it my undivided attention. Then I get in my car to drive where I am meeting Blake for lunch. The entire time I am with him, all I can think about is getting home to read that letter.

"Delilah," I suddenly hear him say, "I have been thinking about this for a while, and I think we should move in together."

I almost choke on an ice cube while sipping my drink when he finishes his suggestion. "Wow," I tell him. "That is a huge step. I've never lived with anyone before."

Blake replies, "Just think about it, no rush on the answer. I want it to also feel right for you."

"Thank you. I will think about it," I say with a smile.

Lunch ends up leading to a small outing downtown. By the time we get back to our cars, the sun is almost down, and the moon is already shining. We then lean in to give each other a kiss before parting ways for the night.

Too busy thinking about what Blake had asked me earlier, I forgot all about the letter that has been waiting in my drawer all day until just now. I have no idea what I am going to do as far as moving in with him is concerned, but first things first. I need to read Damon's letter.

FIFTEEN

After getting into bed, I open the drawer to my nightstand and pull out the envelope with much anticipation. Even though the words couldn't have been written any clearer, I still find myself confused as I read:

> Dear Delilah,
> I would have said something to you sooner, but I wanted to make sure I received final confirmation before saying anything. I want you to be the first to know that I will be home in three weeks—for good. I hope we can get together and catch up once I'm back.
>
> > Excited to see you,
> > Damon

He's coming home? For good? I guess I knew this would happen eventually. But I guess I never really put much thought into what that would mean. One thing is for sure: he needs to be nothing other than OK that I am with Blake. Things are not allowed to be awkward between two men who are both very important to me.

Dear Damon,

That is such exciting news! I bet you can't wait to be back in your own bed after so long. I will have to let you know when Blake and I are available for lunch.

Excited to see you too,
Delilah

I probably shouldn't have written about my current boy-friend in a letter, but in all our communication, Damon still hasn't asked about him. And the last thing I want Damon to think of when he comes home is us starting where we left off. I have to tell him somehow in case he has plans in mind.

Several days later Mrs. Ross decides to call me instead of her usual afternoon text. Before picking up the phone, I already have a feeling I know what it is about. "He's coming home!" she shouts, nearly blowing out my eardrum.

Pretending like I haven't a clue, I respond, "He is? Oh, Mrs. Ross, that's so exciting!"

"It is!" she screeches. "I am going to throw a wel-come-home party for him at my house right when he gets back."

My heart involuntarily sinks, for I know she is going to expect me to be there. "That sounds perfect." I tell her hes-itantly. A welcome-home party truly does sound like a great idea. I'm just not really mentally prepared to see him yet.

"I need your help setting it up." she says, giving me no choice.

"I'm your girl, Mrs. Ross." I tell her before we end the call.

"Fabulous," I say to myself sarcastically.

On the day of the party, I am over at Mrs. Ross's house early for the decoration process. I bought some military airplane decals to stick and hang from the ceiling along with American flags to put in the front lawn leading to the doorway. I also put together a playlist of everything he and I used to listen to in his truck. He always had some form of Texas country song on the radio, so I added all types of different bands to the mix.

The party kicks off, and Damon is running late as usual. Some things never change. I don't expect anything less at this point. I make sure to mingle with everyone whom I haven't met before while being proactive about sipping water. This is to avoid getting dry mouth from being so nervous about seeing him again.

As I am lost in conversation with a gentleman he has apparently served with in the past, sunlight suddenly beams in from the front door and catches my attention. I turn to look and see who it is, but the light is so blindingly bright that all I can see is a tall and broad silhouette hovering in the doorway for a split second before entering. Once the door closes, I regain my eyesight and see Damon.

I try to look away to seem more nonchalant about seeing him again, but I am unable. My breath becomes shallow, and my heart feels like it is racing so fast that it's burning away into nothing. He spots me almost instantly once the door closes, and he begins making his way toward me. I want to run to him and away from him at the same time. Remembering I'm with Blake, I keep my composure to the best of my ability. I only hope it's enough to mask my anxiousness.

Before saying anything, Damon lifts me in the air, giving me the world's tightest hug. It lasts so long as if he hasn't seen me in years and doesn't want to put me down. To be honest I won't be entirely mad if he chooses not to. Once my feet touch the floor again, we formally greet each other.

"It is so nice to see you," he says gratefully.

"It's really nice to see you. It's been too long," I say back, smiling.

He nods and says, "It has."

I take a seat at the kitchen island, and he remains standing next to me, thinking of words to say. He keeps looking at me and then away before there is an awkward silence. I also cannot think of any words. I am too busy fighting off this intense vibe that is taking over my thoughts and the entire house.

"Where is Blake?" he asks.

"Oh," I respond, "he had to work, but we have dinner plans later. He is bummed that he can't be here." That's the truth. I did try to invite him.

Damon is about to say more, but his friend to whom I was talking as he walked in is calling him over. I stay in my seat for a while and see him keeping his eyes on me as he catches up with his military buddy. They both walk by me to get a couple of drinks from the fridge. I notice Damon staring me up and down, looking like he has animalistic intentions as he walks by my chair. My mind is also wandering at this point, but that's OK as long as I give it a short leash and keep it a fantasy. The sexual tension between us becomes too intense, so I get up from my seat to walk out to the back patio to talk with other party guests. The weather outside is perfect, so all the doors are propped open. Even though he is standing behind me inside the doorway leading to the backyard, I can feel his eyes still glued to me.

Along with feeling the need to retreat, I end up drinking too much water, so I walk back inside to use the restroom located down the hall away from the party next to the bedrooms. After washing my hands and fixing my hair in the mirror, I take a step back along with a deep breath, giving myself a pep talk. "You can do this, Delilah. He means nothing to you. Nothing!"

I open the door, and Damon is standing on the other side, waiting for me to come out. As soon as I take my first step, he gently grabs me by the arm and says, "We need to talk," and leads me to a spare bedroom so we can be alone before I can say anything.

He closes the door behind us and stands me up against the wall before leaning in. He places his hands on the wall on each side of my head. Then he says, "Enough tiptoeing, Delilah. I know you feel it too."

Feeling my chest tighten for a moment at the accusation, I respond, "I don't know what you're talking about, Damon. I am here to welcome you home, and that is all. I am with Blake. Understand this."

With slight frustration in his face, he says, "I can't understand it. Tell me you don't love me, Delilah. Tell me I mean nothing to you."

I pause and stare at him for a moment, also beginning to feel frustrated. "You mean a lot to me, Damon. You know that. What we had before, though, is gone."

"I don't believe that, not one bit," he sharply responds before continuing, "You know you want me. Come back to me."

My eyes flood as I tell him, "It's not that simple, Damon. Blake loves me. He would never leave me like you did."

Looking me in the eyes more serious than ever, he demands, "Tell me he gets you going the way I do. Tell me you are in love with him."

Getting defensive, I reply, "He is a good man, and he makes me happy."

Shaking his head, he replies, "Then why can't you tell me you love him?"

I am so flustered that I can't help but scream, "You left! You have no business interfering with my love life!"

Damon angrily steps forward, grabbing my shoulders, making sure my eyes see his. "Damn it, Delilah! I will never leave you alone again! I love you. I have loved you long before meeting you at Emma's pool party, just by all the stories she would tell."

I look at him for a moment and think back at all the stories Emma also told me of him before us meeting. Every ounce of anger I am feeling in this moment melts away as I come to the same realization that I, too, have loved him just as long. But I can't tell him that. "You can't be telling me this, Damon. It doesn't change anything," I tell him sternly.

He steps even closer, and his entire body briefly trembles as he pulls me in and gives me the most passionate kiss. It is way better than any fantasy I could have thought of. I melt into it and end up getting so caught up in it that I don't even realize my eyes are watering. What am I doing? I am with Blake. And we are having dinner in an hour!

I slowly push him away and shake my head as I tell him, "I have to get going."

He looks at me, perplexed. "You're still going?"

I'm not sure what to tell him. I am trying to process all this myself. All I can say is, "This is too much. I need time to think," before I walk toward the exit. I turn the knob to open the front door but not before he grabs me, lifting me for another hug just like the one he gave me when he arrived, a hug making me want to stay right here, just like this, in his arms.

"Take all the time you need. Again, I'm not going any-where," he reassures before setting me back down.

I take off, almost running, before I can change my mind about meeting Blake for dinner. Shortly after driving off in my car, a message from Damon comes through. I wait until I am at a red light before reading it.

"What are you going to do?" he asks. I know what he's really asking is, who am I going to choose? I don't respond to his message. The truth is I don't know. Who I want and who is good for me are, right now, two different things. Damon could possibly be the best damn thing to ever happen to me, but I wouldn't know because he left when we were just getting started. Blake is good for me in every way and always has been.

The rest of the drive, I can't stop thinking about Damon and our conversation. He loves me? How do I feel about Blake? That was honestly a good question on his part. Blake is everything. He marks off anything I might have on a checklist regarding the perfect man. He is drop-dead gorgeous, is fun to be around, genuinely makes me feel loved and important, and the list goes on. He does everything right, and I can see us having a future together. I can see him being a safe person to love. But do I love him?

The restaurant has complimentary valet, so I take full advantage. Once I step out of my car, handing my keys over in exchange for the ticket, I make my way up the steps to the entrance. Blake is already inside at the hostess stand, waiting for me. He takes hold of my hand as we are shown to our reserved table by the pond.

We carry on a usual conversation as we look over the menu, waiting for our cocktails to come. All through dinner neither of us say much as we focus on our meals. The food is so mouthwatering that it's hard to get a word in between each bite. I begin noticing by his mannerisms that he is feeling nervous about something as he finishes the last couple of pieces off his plate. He's fidgeting and looking more at the pond while talking to me than he did previously.

Just after the check arrives at our table, I ask, "Is everything OK?"

He deflects my question by asking one himself, saying, "You didn't mention anything about the party all evening. How was it?"

Pausing for a moment, I realize that he's right. I have been trying so hard not to think of Damon that I blocked out the rest of the party as well. "Oh, it was fun! Everyone was happy to see Damon back home," I respond.

"Well, that's good! I'm glad you had fun," he says before continuing, "Have you thought more about moving in with me?" His eyes are lighting up.

I knew there was something on his mind. I stare at my water glass for a moment as I think of my answer. All I can think of is Damon. I was told once to never think with your brain or your heart because they will contradict each other. To avoid this a person must always listen to what their gut is trying to tell them. Right now everything I have is screaming for Damon—my heart, my brain, my gut, all of it. I have made my decision, so I take a deep breath.

My voice stutters as I regrettably answer him, "I…I am not able to."

"Why is that? Did I move too fast?" he asks.

I waste no time to answer. "No. You didn't."

"What is it then?" he asks desperately.

I reply, "Blake, you are exactly what I need in every way. I care so much about you." Then I pause for a moment before finishing with "But I'm not able to love you the way you deserve. I am sorry."

He leans back, wearing a mask of anger to cover the fact that I have just shattered his heart. I cannot tell if he is trying to find words or not while he stares at the napkin on the table, so I say, "It's killing me that I'm hurting you. I am such a terrible person."

Still looking down, Blake's troubled face melts into a brief smile before looking up to me. "No, Delilah. You are a wonderful person."

Those words make all the tears I am trying to hold back burst into streams down my face. He tells me to take care of myself before paying the bill and taking his leave. Staying in my chair for a moment to finish my wine, I watch him walk away from me for the last time. I can honestly say that I never saw any of this coming. I never thought for a moment that I would have to make this difficult decision. My face falls into my hands with a napkin to absorb the tears.

SIXTEEN

It's been three days since I broke things off with Blake. I haven't talked to Damon or even looked at my phone much for that matter. For the most part, I have been lying in bed and ordering in pizza, wa ching whatever series on television that catches my attention. I've been wanting to reach out to Damon, but I still feel so confused about everything. One part of me feels entirely sure of my choice, but the other part keeps questioning if I have made the right decision. I haven't heard a word from Blake, and to be honest, I don't plan to. His face said enough before getting up from the table.

I wait for the rest of the week to pass before texting Damon, "Meet me at the town lake at noon."

He responds seconds later, saying, "I will be there."

As I put myself together, I don't know what I'm going to say to him. I do know one thing, and that is that I'm going to look good no matter what comes out of my mouth. I throw on a flowy white cotton dress with some one-inch wedge heels and, of course, curl my hair, parting it in the middle.

Literally catching every red light, I make it to the lake about a quarter past noon. As I park my car, I can see him out on the walking bridge that crosses from one side of the lake and leads to the other. He must have seen me pull in because he is fully facing my direction, waiting for me to get out of the car.

He doesn't have to wait long because, as soon as I turn it off, I unbuckle my seat belt and run toward him, leaving the car door open, forgetting all my things on the passenger seat. When I'm about ten feet away, I see his shoulders drop, and he throws out his arms for me to jump in. As I come in for the touchdown, I maintain my speed, making him do a spin from the momentum upon catching me in the air. After completing a 360 spin, he places me back down, still wrapping his arms around me, as I tell him, "I love you. I've always loved you. And I will always love you."

He lifts me back in his arms, leaving only the tips of my toes on the ground, as he says, "I am never letting you go. I promise."

Then we give each other one of those long and memorable kisses that are seen in the movies. The breeze is blowing just enough to lift my curls off my back, giving them a little tangle at the ends. The occasional whiffs of his cologne are making a lasting impression as they embed themselves in my memory of this moment. Walking hand in hand, we take our time walking around the lake, catching up on each other's lives from when we were apart. This is one of those man-made lakes in the middle of a city park. So the walk is more than doable but still works up an appetite.

Afterward we go to a lunch spot that is about a two-minute drive away. He begins telling me about all the places he has traveled while serving in the military. "Gosh," I say, "I would be happy to see half of those places if I could."

"Let's do it!" he eagerly responds. "I'll plan everything. You just worry about packing."

"Nothing to complain about there!" I say before pausing to think. "Let's put Havasu Falls on the list too. There is something I need to do there."

I can tell he is curious, but he decides not to ask probably because he likes surprises almost as much as I do. "Done," he says.

Only two weeks later, he drops by my place with a list of places he wants to take me to. He even has a full itinerary for each location. Finally, here is someone who can plan trips to my approval. I eagerly look down the list and catch Havasu Falls as spot number three. I point to it and say, "This one may take a while to get into. You need a permit and a campground reservation."

"Done and done," he replies with a smile before continuing, "The soonest availability they had for this trip is a year out.

"Wow! What can we get done in a year?" I ask rhetorically.

He takes advantage of the opportunity by answering, "Oh, I have a few ideas. After all, we have to make up for lost time."

And we definitely did. He had planned a new adventure for us almost every week, whether it was something as extravagant as a hot-air balloon ride or as simple as fishing in a nearby canal. The idea was to make as many memorable experiences as possible. We knocked several items off my bucket list as well like visiting the pink side of the Great Salt Lake in Utah and walking through the Imperial Sand Dunes, located roughly twenty miles west of Yuma, Arizona.

We've been to enough places and shared memories to almost fill up a photo album. We have it placed on the coffee table in our condo. That's right, we moved in together. We have been living together for the past eleven months, and it has been complete bliss, as perfect of a fit as two missing puzzle pieces finally coming together.

We are a week out from our Havasu Falls trip, and so we tackle the familiar list of items we'll need. There's one thing I plan on adding to that list. I run to our room and open the side table cabinet and come back into the common area holding the wooden box that Mrs. Ross gave me. "What is that?" Damon asks as he looks down at the small box in my hands.

"It's Emma." I pause before continuing in a low voice, "I promised her that we'd see Havasu Falls together." I look down at the box and smile, knowing that soon I'll be able to fulfill that promise.

He smiles back and says, "Here, I'll take her," while holding out his hands. "I'll place her in a safe spot in the truck."

I hand her over before grabbing my bag, following him. We get in, fill up the tank, and drive off toward the Grand Canyon.

As we arrive to the parking lot, I reunite with the memories I made the last time I was here. I can't wait to show Damon the ropes. Maybe I can piggyback on him in the first two miles until we hit flatter territory. He might not even notice.

We start making our way down the trail while I tell him all about each passing waterfall as we get closer to the campground. Havasu Falls, in all its might, catches Damon's attention the most as it did mine.

"I want to come back here tomorrow morning," I tell him as I point to the rushing waterfall.

"Deal," he agrees before asking, "And then what would you like to do?"

"I think we should tackle Mooney Falls," I suggest before continuing, "I hear it's quite the adventure."

"Let's do it," he says, excited, up for the challenge.

The next morning we pack enough supplies to be gone the entire day, even extra for emergencies. I pack the box with Emma in my sack as well. Then we make our way to Havasu Falls. The wind picks up just enough to cool us down as we hike up toward the waterfall. Once we arrive, we both take a seat near the pool to catch our breath while we dangle our feet in the water.

I open my bag and pull out the little wooden carved box. Damon reaches his hand over and places it on top of my hands. I look down as I say, "I miss her so much, Damon. It's been so hard."

"I know what you mean, Delilah. She was my best friend too," he says. "She's still here."

I stand up, with him following my lead. The wind blows harder as I respond, "And now she always will be." I open the box to let the breeze take her away. Damon pulls me in just in time for my first teardrop to fall on his shoulder. He takes his hand and wipes the second tear away before coming in to kiss me.

"You know I love you?" he asks.

"I do," I tell him, smiling.

"Good. Let's get to Mooney Falls. The map says it's about one mile away from here," he eagerly replies.

We walk the path through the Havasupai Campground leading to the Mooney Falls trailhead. A little way down the trailhead, we can see the two-hundred-foot waterfall from a bird's-eye view. We both stop for a few minutes to admire the sight of the rushing waters gliding down the travertine walls.

"Well," Damon says, "should we descend down to the bottom?"

"Absolutely!" I tell him without hesitating.

We make our way to the small cave leading to the slippery, wobbly ladders that we will be climbing down. On the way to the cave's opening, I read a warning sign that says, "Descend at your own risk." It's a good thing we are wearing proper shoes because this looks utterly difficult.

We both grab hold of the chains that are bolted in the wall as we walk through the cave and down some stairs. Eventually, the stairs come to an end, and the fearful ladders begin to taunt me. Damon goes first since he is the more experienced one. Besides, I am afraid of heights at times. The very first thing I do once I start descending is look down unintentionally through my feet toward the ground. I freeze for a moment before taking a deep breath while returning my attention to the part of the ladder in front of my face. Then I watch my hands while they move one after the other as I climb down. Before I know it, the chain ladders end, and there's a short stack of wooden ones right before the bottom. As I take my first steps onto these ones, they seem even more slippery than the chains, but at least if I fall now, my survival rate is higher than before.

After Damon reaches the bottom, he waits to guide me by my waist when I am two steps from reaching the ground. We both take a step back and look up at the tall, blue-green waters. "Last one in is a swamp rat!" Damon yells as he takes off his shirt and runs toward the water.

"First one in has to eat it!" I respond while hopping, struggling to take off my other shoe.

He makes it first by a split second only because he has cheated. Eventually, we are both in the waters, holding each other, kissing some more, and laughing. This moment along with the entire day is absolutely perfect. We play and cool off for a bit longer in the seventy-degree Fahrenheit geothermal pool before making our way back out of Mooney Falls toward the lodge.

The stars are out, shining brighter than ever, along with a full moon. There is a slight breeze, so we are wrapped up together in a big blanket. We decide to sit out in front of the lodge, admiring the sky and the rest of our surroundings.

Suddenly, Damon unwraps himself from the blanket before standing up. Wondering what he's doing, I keep eyes on him. Then I see him pull something small and shiny out of his pocket before getting down on one knee. His face is inches from mine. He holds up a ring in between our hearts and says, "Delilah, I have literally traveled all over the world. Having a place in your life has been my favorite destination. I want the rest of my adventures with you. I need you in my life forever. Will you marry me?"

After covering my face with my hands, I then jump out of the blanket onto him, knocking him over to the ground. I fall on top of him and kiss him repeatedly as I cry, "Yes, yes, I'll marry you! Yes!" He places the engagement ring on my finger, and I throw my arms around him as he then carries me inside. We strip off the little clothing we have on after showering the day off us and get under the covers. Before falling asleep, we consummate the engagement.

The morning sun lets us know bright and early that it is time to wake up and head on home, closing out this adventure. I am looking forward to adding all these photos to the album. We've had so many wonderful memories in one trip.

SEVENTEEN

Two months later after returning from Havasu Falls, I am not feeling too well. Walking to the kitchen for a glass of water, I start to feel nauseous. I change direction, running to the bathroom and making it to the toilet before vomiting. After wiping my mouth before flushing, I get up and walk over to the mirror. I look at my pale reflection as I try to think of what I may have eaten that made my stomach so upset. Moments later it hit me. I stare in shock at my reflection as I realize I am a whole week late for my period.

I quickly drive to the nearby convenient store to buy a pregnancy test while Damon is out in a job interview. On the way to the store and back home, I am guzzling down water. Once inside the condo, I rush to the bathroom while tearing the pregnancy test box open, leaving pieces on the floor. I pee on the stick for as long as the instructions say to before placing it flat on the counter. Now I wait in complete agony while counting the minutes for the results to appear.

I have to walk away momentarily to compose myself. The timer goes off, and I make my way back to the bathroom and look on the counter. There it is, that pink plus sign as vibrant as ever, indicating a positive. I'm pregnant.

My breathing stops as I fall into a slight panic attack before I catch my inner voice, yelling, "Breathe! The baby needs oxygen! This is no longer about you! Get over it!" Then I start gasping for air until I fully catch my breath.

Now I think of how to share the news with Damon. We've had the whole kids talk before, but we never delve too deeply into it, probably because we both figure it is still so far away. But the time has come. I feel extremely nervous about how he may take the news, but I'm also excited.

I call Mrs. Ross for advice. "Oh, Delilah! I am going to be a grandma!" is the first thing she shouts.

That's not entirely helpful, but it does ease my mind a lot, so I guess it does help in a way. I ask, "But, Mrs. Ross, how do I tell him?"

She pauses for a moment before giving me her words of wisdom. "Honey, it doesn't really matter how you tell him. It's there either way, and he'll be happy all the same."

"How do you know that?" I question.

She answers with certainty, "He loves you, baby, and he'll love everything you two make together."

Talking to Mrs. Ross gives me the confidence I need to tell Damon. As soon as I end the call with her, I scroll through my contacts for his name. I take one more deep breath before calling.

I hear two rings before he answers, "Hey, Delilah, what's going on?"

I reply, "I have some exciting news to tell you tonight."

Sounding confused about what it might be, he answers, "OK, I can't wait to hear!"

"Perfect," I tell him. "I'll order in dinner."

Shortly after he arrives, I place pasta and salad at the table along with an unopened bottle of wine. Liquid courage is rumored to help in times like these. Of course, I won't be having any. So I'm not entirely sure how helpful it will be this time.

I bring our plates to the kitchen sink before sitting back down at the table with him. Then I slide a small white box over in front of him tied with a yellow bow. I remain quiet as he looks up to me before untying the ribbon. He lifts the top off, revealing a set of white baby socks along with a note saying, "2 + 1 = 3."

He slowly places the box down on the table and lifts the socks out, holding them for a moment in his hand while staring at them. The silent anticipation is keeping me on edge. Before my nerves can once again stop my breathing, he looks up at me and smiles. He stands up from his chair so fast and pulls me up from mine. He holds me as he kisses my face all over, coming back to my lips for the finish.

"I'm going to be a daddy?" he says with excitement while his eyes fill with water.

"I have an appointment next week to confirm the due date, but it should be sometime in September," I tell him.

"Delilah," he says, "this is the best news!"

A few months pass, bringing us to June, our wedding month. My belly is getting bigger, and my clothes are feeling tighter. I would like to say I carry it well, but pregnancy is hard work. It is not for the weak, that's for sure. Running around, trying to get the rest of the wedding stuff all organized, has me even more winded than it would if I were my normal size. It doesn't help much that I am pregnant during the hottest months of the year. Simply describing it as hot is an understatement. Thank goodness Mrs. Ross is, for the most part, taking the lead on everything. She may just be more excited for this wedding than I am, which is hard to fathom.

I had suggested to Damon that the town lake would be the perfect spot for the wedding. It has a strong hold on me already because that was where Damon and I officially reunited. Plus, it's a pretty scenic place with its multiple bridges, rows of trees, a stone walking path circling the entire perimeter, and of course all the dense, green summer grass covering just about everything else. We both agreed to a smaller wedding, keeping the guest list to only family and close friends.

I have picked out a simple, long, and white wedding dress barely loose enough to hide my baby bump. It is silk with lace cut-outs in various places, tapering to the ground. I don't feel the need for a train or veil; I plan on braiding flowers in my hair instead.

The day of the wedding is here, and I am filling with anxiety. I am so nervous that I am sure I'm going to be sick. I have Mrs. Ross to put me together as well as my mom. She is finally feeling well enough to start venturing out of the house again. For a while she couldn't sit or stand long without being in pain. Other than undergoing rehabilitation to make her stronger, she is, for the most part, resting in bed. It means the world to me that she can make it here today.

I hear the bridal entrance music, signaling that it is time for me to walk down the stone path toward a natural arch made by two trees where Damon is standing, waiting for me. As I approach I catch him wiping a tear from under his right eye, not taking his eyes off me. Once again, everyone else disappears but him and me. I'm pretty sure I just about float away as well. I snap back to present when it is time for me to say "I do" before sealing it with a kiss. Then we celebrate by dancing the night away full of laughs, smiles, and more memories to finish the photo album chronicling our love story.

September arrives, and the baby comes a week early. One moment we are rushing to the hospital, and a few hours later, our baby girl is delivered and in Damon's arms while I take a breather. Mrs. Ross and my mom are the first to stop by with an abundant number of balloons and flowers. After Mrs. Ross sets them in the corner and helps my mom to a nearby seat, she walks over to us and peers down at the baby. "A beautiful baby girl," she says before asking, "What is her name?"

I look at Damon holding the most precious thing I've ever seen. He carefully passes her off into Mrs. Ross's arms. She looks down at the baby with all the love in the world she has to offer accompanied by tears as I tell her, "Emma. Her name is Emma."

Printed in the USA
CPSIA information can be obtained
at www.ICGtesting.com
JSHW010938220224
57591JS00007B/164